I0831596

The First Book:

From the Ridge

ISBN: 978-0-615-26192-8

This will be my first “stab” as it were, into the field of published back slapping and heavy handed hand kissing and baby shaking. Or maybe that’s backwards…

I was first attempting to write only a book of fiction. Short fiction actually, because of an irritating segment in a Stephen King book of all places. In it he states that the art of the short story is a dying beast. An animal that’s too difficult and possibly too tenuous to be able to grasp onto fully for the author. At first I thought, “MAN! You suck Stevie! I can’t believe you of all people say that crap! I’m injured in my places of injury I tell ya!” I was aghast. I thought he had lost the truth of it, that short fiction was the way to the heart and the juicy meaty places of all people. I thought he was merely done with the real and his ghost writers (cuz no one man can write THAT much, can he?) were slacking off in their jobs. But no, this was written out of knowledge that I didn’t, or more to the point wouldn’t, listen to. To me, the novel is the enemy, at least at this point in my fledgling career as a writer of sorts. I’ve been doing it, like most of our destitute and lonely breed, for most of my life. But it took me a hell of a long assed time to get to the point where I was comfortable with my life path. Life path. Huh. Sounds like a feel good seminar. But it’s the truth; it’s the path that, for better or worse, I need to be on. I ran from that truism for about twenty eight years and realized that I could continue to work ten jobs a year, of I could buckle down and get to it.

All this time I've been on the fourteen year two year degree plan (did I mention I'm a serious procrastinator?) and am at the moment of possible completion. Just that last friggin math class to go, and of course an English class. In my case slow and steady won't win the race, in fact I don't even think the race is still going. Those folks that started with me on that run down the halls of academe have, I think, since ran to the finish, got their trophies and have moved out to the Midwest to raise sheep. No clue where they are. But I'm still going, and to me that's the most important thing to remember.

So since this is my first introduction to any book ever, (and I think this is mine…) I have no idea what to write. I could traipse around in a Goth kinda thing, stroking the fear as stevie do, but I won't. Not really my style, though I always loved the "touch here in the dark dear reader" thing he always does. Man, that dude KNOWS how to creep out an audience. And maybe I will creep you out, dear reader, for you are all dear to me. Without the reading populace at large, freaks like me wouldn't have a thing to do. We'd huddle in our rooms/apartments/turnpikes and cackle to ourselves about people that exist only in our minds and the weird things we can do to them.

It's funny, when I finally understood the freak status I was born with, I went to my parents and in a fit of one of those (NO really, I need to tell you) things I let them know. I told them flat out. "Mom. Dad. I want to be a writer." It was like I had whacked em with a hammer. I think if I had told them I wanted to be an actor it would have been less of a blow. At least then I would have a waiting job in a decent restaurant. But of course, I did that gig, and I can't wait tables. I really suck and if I had to live by my tips I'd be dead.

So ten years after this startling realization and coming out of the writing closet to my parents, I start my writing "career" the way I want to. I take all the tons and reams and notes and papers and place them all in a HUGE compendium, that number something like thirty pages. Hmmmff… Not good enough. So then I decided to take all the stuff I had written for my website, fromtheridge.com by the way in case you haven't heard of it, and so I did that and low and behold, sixty pages.

Damn it! Still not enough.

So the dream, the start of this magnanimous historic first book would not be a book solely of short stories like I wanted, nor be a book of only writing from the website on weird crap I've done and my take on the world at large, but hell, why not do it all? Since I've been a Gemini/Taurus cusp baby for my whole life, why not do it like my life has always been done? Except finishing it, that would be a change and a half.

So here it is, my first brain baby. I have no idea whether it's a boy or a girl. I think it's more of a changeling thing, small but growing, hungry maybe. And maybe that's how my career will go, small at first, but growing. Always growing.

And maybe it's hungry as well.

Christopher R. Ridge

6/2/2008

Los Osos, California

Contents

Short Fiction

Poetry

Travels

Essays

Short Fiction

Alright! The first one and fresh off the presses. Come on, smell it. The fresh smell of inked print. It usually reminds me of grade school. The old mimeograph in the office. The one we waited for. When the teacher whipped out that paper, there was a collective sigh that went through the room, and for no other reason then to smell that paper.

But hey, let's go over here....

On the Subject of Berries

We start above a city. Any city will do, but its gotta be near the woods. Big woods. Woods that stretch for days and days.

The kids come over the ridge. They've been trying to reach it for over an hour, and the rest is taken with total abandon. Packs are dropped to the ground, with a groan from some quarters, and they sit. The four have been friends for ever to them, bout 4 years to the rest of us of any seasoning. They bask in the sun, filtered through the large pines that dot the landscape, and close their eyes.

Thoughts begin to drift.

The first one to truly start the epidemic begins to see the patterns. He's slightly surprised, but allows himself to succumb to the quartered glyphs and basic geometric shapes.

At this point in our story, dear reader, the game is lost; the towel has been thrown in. The children are lost.

The first, eldest by 22 minutes, opens his eyes. He sees before them, on the trail to where they are, a bush of berries. They look somewhat like holly berries, but larger. The leaf structure is more succulent, as if in times of need the plant can survive on limited water and persevere.

He sits staring at the plant for quite some time, the others are still daydreaming. They rock to the patterns behind their eyes. Some hum while they rock.

The eldest, Mr. 22, stands up and stretches, in constant view to the plant. He watches it with a singular intensity, an intensity that is all consuming.

As he watches, the berries begin to scintillate. They through off sparks like a strange ornament lit from behind on a Christmas tree. It begins to rotate slowly, first left, then right. It doesn't seem to follow the arc of the sun, doesn't respond to the wind. Its stock still.

He's now in front of the plant. If he had wanted to confront the lapse of time felt while gazing at the plant he would find he has no recollection of the time between rising and the walk to the plant, a mere ten to fifteen feet away. But he doesn't. The plant is his all.

A couple of others have begun to come around to his movement and the source of it. They become enthralled.

The first is one again first in things of the mountain this day. He bends over and ever so tenderly, plucks a berry. In his hand it shines like a light, but in broad daylight. This is in no way unusual to the youth, and the others are now there. Bending. Picking. He, the first, the eldest, is barely ahead of the others as they eat the singular berry that they each have now in their hand.

After they got home, trying to suspend the monumental thing they had done, they fell asleep. The sleep was deep and total. As their breathing slowed, and the changes began, they felt no pain as the bones shifted, and the change overcame them.

As one, almost with an instinctual need they arise. As their heightened senses take in their surroundings they sense others with those environments. The others are perceived, to those poor youths, as older, frailer, weaker.

It doesn't start as a hunter prey scenario, that’s not the driving force of these feral creatures. They need no sustenance. Their only drive, the drive given to them not mere hours before, is the drive to mark, maim, and immerse themselves in the older blood. To impregnate them.

Hours later the paramedics called to the first scene that will soon become a well known facet of a crumbling society, the precursor of the epidemic, are the strange succulents growing from the victims. The children of these people are never found, but at all the sites other children from the neighborhoods, where the original mountain walkers lived, where all found roaming about the site.

And every single other child was eating some sort of berries.

These transcripts were translated from the original Gaelic of the author. These pages were found in an attic in the Canadian province of Quebec and were found after the renovation of a Victorian era house.

Being the Honest and Truthful Accounting of my Capture and Time Amongst the Heathen of Western New England

On how I came to be captured

This is my, Christian Mac Iomaire's, personal recollection of the time I spent with the Penobscot tribes of Maine. It is truthful and honest and is sworn so before the Goddess and the God of my Druidic forefathers.

I, being strong of will and stature, reflect upon that time with great trepidation and only my strength of will can withstand the buckling of my legs leading me down upon the floor of this place. The truth of my sitting upon the chair restricts this possibility and encourages, even allows me to continue upon my telling of my trials.

As I was a strong and adventurous youth I entered into servitude for a British gentleman and his family of the name of Cornekey. As they were not at all abusive or abhorrent to me, I was inclined to venture with them to the New World and seek my fortune after the agreed upon seven years of service I was to give them. I left my family, with wishes from both mine father and mother to write often and try to retain a dwelling for them as well when able, and ventured across the sea to the west of that great island and away from my loving and sheltering Ireland.

The seas were unkind yet navigable and we made it there with few lives lost. Most were of the poor ships crew and their brethren, sucked over by the fierce and unaccommodating seas. Till the ends of my days and beyond I shall forever be in debt to those brave men whom gave up their lives for our safe passage. We landed in the port of Boston and began immediately to travel to the north. As we traveled the hills and vales began to rise much higher and mightier into the skies and the farms and hamlets began to fade into the wooded areas. Yet before our arrival at our supposed destination we were beset upon by the natives of the tribe known as Penobscot as I was later to learn from them. The family, Mr. and Mrs. Cornekey and all of their children were slaughtered and their scalps were taken. The blows were not unlike the sounds of melons being thrown from a cart, crushing upon the ground. The natives were, however, quite skilled in their endeavor and didn't cause the brains to be spilt at all. For some reason the rest of the servants, myself included, were not in any way harmed, though we were bound and gagged and led off into the forest away from the track we were once following.

On where we were led and how we were treated

As we moved deeper into the forest and farther from the civilization I was adapted to, the trees and forest began to change and become much more verdant and wild. Our captors seemed to be at their leisure within the coniferous confines and strode with little or no effort. The women that were captives had the most trouble, though slightly less troubled were the men. The foot wear devised by the fashionable in Paris were not created for the harsh travels we were now inclined to persevere. As I had been raised within the wilds of Ireland and had been bare of foot for lack of money for shoes I soon doffed my thick-soled high-lows that had been purchased when we had arrived in Boston and reverted back to my essential roots of walking. As soon as I did that however I was beaten by the one native I beheld as the leader of the band and had my shoes shoved back into my face. As my arms were bound behind my back and I was unable to withstand the blows given me, I agreed with nod of head and put on the dreaded things again. I wished for a knife, not to do violence but to be able to alter the shoes for better wearing in such rough terrain.

After walking for three hours of the clock we stopped for a short rest. There we also met up with another group of natives coming from, as near as I could tell the same direction we had come from. From the captives in that group we found out that the tribe had moved en masse against the city of New York and had slaughtered and raised much of that great city to the ground. Many of the captives wept upon hearing of the destruction of New York and began to ply the other captives for information about their families or the areas that their families were in, but to no avail. They had not the news to give, nor were they allowed the chance to give it. In reverence to the dead I gave offerings to the four directions and to the god and goddess and asked that the departed were allowed an easy passage to the other world. Many of the captives being of the Christian persuasion shunned me after this, yet the natives that witnessed it showed great consternation and agitation and took me away from the group of other captives. The other captives were sent off with the main group of natives and I was taken with the original group that had attacked and slaughtered the Cornekey's. The other captives went east and we, the natives and I, went in a northern direction.

On How I Learned Their Speech

As we walked, always northern in direction, I began to learn their language. Slowly at first then quicker as the smaller and easier words began to build on the larger and more intricate patterns of their speech. It had been almost a full week of walking and having no chance for any other avenue of interest beyond the forest and its inhabitants; I took to watching the native's interaction with each other. I found it odd that only I had been taken with this party and thought strange and disquieting thoughts. At first I was sure they would kill me out right, yet as time went on and I was treated as well as could be expected I began to notice them noticing me. Always at the times when I was praying in my native Gaelic language or when I was observing certain rituals that were themselves outlawed by the subjugation of the Catholic Church. That same church that had tried to drive out of our women and out of our lives the beliefs that we all had had for generations. They had been the reason and the means for the destruction of our way of life and the death of our last warrior Gaelic queen. I had heard of the subjugation of these people as well, but had as yet seen its direct control over them.

As we moved, always northern, the natives were met again and again by smaller groups of the same tribe or district. The original natives that had taken the large group of captives had been of a different tribe or sect then the natives I was with. As they were joined almost daily by larger and larger parties I began to realize that they were a nation of people and they were on the move. From where and to where I could only guess at, but I was sure they were leaving their home lands for a different area. I neither understood the why of it nor did I understand the where they were going, but only that the *entire nation* of these people were leaving. As it had been three days since my capture and the tribe had grown larger and larger I thought that they would be easier to find. Yet it was incredible the way they moved through the forest. They would travel in groups of no more then fifteen people, yet within sight of at least two to three of the other groups. They traveled with all their possessions carried on their backs and on litters that they would carry between members of the same family within the nation. As I was not used to these dense forests or those pathetic shoes I was constantly traded between the groups probably because my ability to travel as they were was somewhat stinted.

On the second week after I awoke to the cook fires and the noise of an awakened group of people numbering as far as I could tell five thousand or more

I was surprised and dismayed to find my shoes missing. I was also more dismayed at the loss of my clothing, until I noticed some soft leather on the ground of my tent. After I had unraveled the featureless lump of leather I found it to be a garment of the natives themselves including the soft shoes that they wear. I donned the clothing and found it quite comfortable as well as beautiful in its simplistic design. It reminded me of the clothing my ma would make for my brothers and sisters and I. Soft almost featureless yet incredibly durable and pragmatic. That morning I left my tent dressed as a native in clothing, yet closer to them as a nation then the America I was supposedly destined to be a part of. I had no idea if I was even in the colonies any more or if anyone was trying to find me. I use find versus rescue primarily because I was not sure I was truly a captive any more. The natives had loosed my bonds the first day as soon as we had stopped for the evening and had yet to reapply them to me. I think that since we were deep in the woods and not around any colonial areas I would have been unable to go anywhere or even to survive on my own. The removal of my clothing and the giving of theirs was almost a peace offering, especially as soon as I realized it was from the same man that had beaten me when I had removed my shoes on that first day. At this time I had grown slightly less feeble in my attempts to converse with them as I had before and I asked one of the natives passing me where my clothes had been taken. Being the taciturn native he merely pointed to the large cook fire already burning in the center of their make shift village. I would be lying if I said that I was sad of the loss of my Europeans garb, but I was not. The clothing that had replaced it was stronger then the clothing I had lost and better made then it as well.

On my being made free through Induction into the Tribe

My life for the next weeks went on as this one had, always moving, always north, and always switched in between the groups of this strange traveling nation yet not as much as before. I was finding it easier to move through the forest and since that toil was relieving itself of my mind the language barrier was also moving father afield. Day by day I was learning more and more of their nuances and behaviors of speech and communication. I was also gathering a small group of women for some reason. I gathered that they were intrigued by my skin and my way of prayer which as I found out by being with them was not so different from my own. As my religion was more ritual based the natives were more dance based. They believed as I did that our ancestors were not gone to some heavenly church in gods' mansion, but available and accessible to those left behind on the earth.

So it went on; we traveled daily, I was switched less and less and more often then not I was around certain women of the tribe that had shown an interest in me. It was as if the leader, who was the one that supervised the switching of the groups for me, was trying to find a mate for me within the tribe. I realize now that that was what was happening. It started with about seven women, and then shrunk down to three, then down to two. One was a slight, yet fiery woman who was approximately twenty years of age and an older woman who was as far as I could understand it a widow. As I became more prolific in their language I realized that matrimony was the end result of both of these women and was sanctioned by the chief of their tribe. Both were attractive, both were intelligent and both were available, yet being only a young man and not wise in the ways of the world, and as the older woman had a child already from her previous engagement, I was more inclined to pursue the younger woman.

About this time I was instructed by one of the younger warriors in the tribe that the chief wanted to talk to me in his tent. As I was now able to understand the language better then I ever had I went with a clear purpose and knowledge that I could speak with assurance to the chieftain in a manner that would benefit me more then him.

As I entered his tent I realized he had packed and lit his peace pipe and was receiving me with a smile and a greeting of welcome. I was amazed yet assured that I was not on the unequal status that I had been in when I had received at this mans hands a beating for the removal of my shoes.

He was an imposing creature. He had strange alternating patterns down the right side of his face using a marking of blackened paint. His hair, due to the war they had engaged in, was shaved only on the sides and spiked when in battle. But now it was laying quite calmly down the side of his face. His wife was there as well and she greeted me with a much more relaxed and pleasant smile. As he was the chief, and a man of stature and command within the tribe, he was as always very straightforward in his dealings but not one to cut a jibe or joke at another's expense. He was a good man, and on all accounts a gentleman.

He proceeded, after smoking and sharing the pipe with me, to tell me of his wish for my happiness. As he was happy after his marriage and the births of his children, he thought that I would be as well. As this took me aback he noticed the look on my face and was immediately concerned. He thought he had made a mistake and was quick to ask my forgiveness in his blunder, but I told him it was not him. I was unsure where or how I was to live let alone love and provide for a wife not of my nation. At this he laughed and said "Do you not belong to us now?" At this I was stunned and unable to truly reiterate my point. He laughed and asked if I was not of them, they were of me now and able to better understand me then the people I was a "slave" to. I was the one to tell him, before, of my time as an indentured servant and the rules of that engagement and how I had come to be in the company of the Cornekey family. Yet since they were dead, and no one had come to find me, or even knew where I was, I was at a crossroads of decision. Do I slough off all ties to Ireland and my blessed family? Or do I leave to try to find my way back, possibly being killed along the way, or even if I'd be able to acquire the finances to book my own passage to my blessed green tinged isle. I was at a loss and needed to think, so I told him so and retired to my tent.

All that night and all the next morning into the afternoon I wrestled with the problem of my new position. That I was still a captive was a concluded quest upon my intellect, yet was I truly free? Did the servitude I was "freed" from prevent me from seeking solace and help from those that might then again subject me to it? I was in a dilemma and the only way to free myself truly was to remain as dead as I thought the rest of humanity thought me to be. I went again into the chiefs' tent and told him that I was going to stay with them and adopt their ways as my own. He was pleased and asked me whom I felt would most compliment my life with them. As I told him it was with the younger of the women I was acquainted with he smiled and asked someone behind me in the entrance of the tent to come in. She, the younger woman, entered and asked of her father, with a smile for me, what it was he wanted. He asked her if I was the one to compliment her life and she agreed. Two days later we were married and I had been, in one moment freed from bondage and accepted into a new life with a new people.

A DATE WITH D

When I entered the diner, the decor surprised me. The room was about 400 to 600 feet square. The walls were covered by a maroon velvet shag carpet in a bizarre paisley pattern. Along the wall to my left and right were interspersed light fixtures that were metallic silver gray arms extending out to end in hands cradling lit bulbs. I think that they were about thirty watts. Most of the light came from these fixtures within the walls. There were absolutely no forms of lighting on the ceiling. The rest of the dim light came from the tables scattered throughout the place. On them, or more to the point, imbedded in them were the same as on the walls. But in this case the fingers were not cradling the bulbs but grasping them with alternating fist, woman's tender grip, and the very rare child's inquisitive first touch with the bulb suspended by wires to the child's finger. The actual table sizes ranged from small kidney like shapes to a huge amorphous blob that took up a good side corner of the establishment.

As I passed by the lights, they would flicker, ever so slightly, and I paused to see if any human had seen it. Some tables I passed while I followed the gentle but insistent pull in my stomach were occupied. Said occupants would shiver and complain of some air conditioning glitch and shrug on a coat. One man, a slim goatee, dark intense eyes and an air of mystique looked at the space of my wake and was puzzled. That was all. On my way to a date with someone I didn't know I passed the true entrance to the establishment. Without even looking behind me I knew that the wall I had come through was an unbroken line of metallic silver arms reaching out with their gifts of light.

I saw him and knew. Knew that he was the one I had come to collect so I waited. I watched him begin to choke and then it happened. His head kind of did that slow crazy lift with both his fat meaty hands around his own throat. His face began to turn blue when the first concerned citizen showed up on the scene. With that slapping on the back of the aforementioned citizen I realize with amusement that the aforementioned citizen has no medical background or training whatsoever. After the four or fifth pound on the back of my collection, the boy was on the ground. I moved over to the table and saw that it had been a chunk of lobster. All that butter and the poor sod couldn't even get it down. He had never learned the thirty chews your food method of healthy eating.

Someone else appears and begins to clear the throat way, but it's useless. He's on his last oxygen molecule. I reach down and take his crown chakra first. That way he feels no more pain. It's hard enough for me to watch; sometimes the collections are kids, so I learn little ways within the confines of my job description that eases the sufferings of those I meet. It's the least I can do. So after the crown chakra I go down the line and collect all seven and place them carefully in my bag. They are taken for processing later. All that's left is the shell of the chakra. This one appears as an overweight man wearing a red Hawaiian shirt, Birkenstock sandals with socks, ands Bermuda shorts. I don't tarry long. I have others to meet so I leave immediately through the roof and into the night sky over the city in search of that insistent pull that leads me toward the next one. The next one to have a date with D.

IT CAME FROM THE FRIDGE

It stands usually in the corner of the kitchen. An immense white monolith magnetized inherently by the decorations that mob its face. If one more magnet is applied, a magnetilanche could ensue. Or it could begin to draw everything metal in a three-mile radius towards itself like some incredibly rectangular black hole of domestica.

No one's opened the damn thing in thirty-five years. The chains that surround it are rusted ever so slightly, yet are still strong enough for pretty much anything that could come out of it.

The fridge. It stands alone, dusty, no longer plugged in, in the hopes that whatever cleared the stray cats and dogs, rats, cockroaches, flies, bees, children, police, accountants, and everything else would never come again. They could only hope.

If you ask old man Withers he'll tell you that he saw it all, but he's lying. He ran like all the rest of them. Ran behind the freezer, then realizing that they had unwittingly hid in a possible enemy stronghold, leaped to their safety behind the gas range. It had thought them cowed and at the time its assessment had been correct, but they had lulled it for awhile with slabs of sirloin from Ted's butcher shop and had then bought the chains and dropped the whole thing in the river. They had considered the matter closed.

It had reopened their respective matters and refrigerator doors.

Johnathan was the one that suggested that they burn it when it came again, so they had waited with Molotov cocktails and homemade napalm but it had tricked them and was behind in the freezer. It crawled out and grabbed Bill first, but since Bill was an asshole the others didn't mind so much. They scattered while it molded and digested him, the fingers of his left hand still reaching long after his face had been molded and destroyed, sucked back into the baked potato that was its makeshift mouth. Ted couldn't take his eyes off of the maraschino cherries that seemed to glare at him from just under the macaroni and cheese eyebrows. The body was a difficult thing to describe, so I won't. Plus most of them are dead now, so I think that in respect I should just end it there. If you want more, ask Mr. Wither's about it. He'll tell you a story of adventure, intrigue, espionage, and love.

(Later with Mr. Withers.)

It came out that last time and we burned it. We burned it for Johnny, for Edith, for my little Norma Jean schnauzer Poofty, for Delilah, for Chuck, for Dave, for Tilly, for Gertie, for Dook boy, for Corkscrew, and for Slimy Pete. It came out looking like a Celtic ceremony that spent too many days without proper refrigeration. Dook had leaked out the Freon and we had waited for three days. It was in June, and we did them three days without cold water mind you. We waited, sucking down warm beers, and when it showed itself we torched it like a bad bunch of hay gone wild. We still had the napalm made from black powder, kerosene, and dishwashing liquid. I had a couple of them ready and let loose as Ted threw on his lucky Zippo. It went up, we got out. I know for a fact that the ones of us that survived never owned another refrigerator again. Never again. That's all there is to it boy, so beat it. I'm done talkin'.

Suffering

I destroyed a brilliant light of life. An actual piece of beauty and love. I destroyed this bright shining being in an instant, and I got off scot free. A night in jail was all I got. Wow. Big deal. Like a damn nights going to change anything. He's dead. The little boys dead. Smashed in an instant. 3000 pounds of steel traveling 90 miles an hour hit him. He never had a chance. All I saw was what looked like a bike, and then the red was on the windshield. That was probably the worst. Not the sound of the bike being dragged under the car. Not the crunch of his frail little bones snapping as he flew at the windshield. Just the red. The wash of red as his head cracked against my shatter proof glass spewing his not yet knowledged brains all over the windshield and hood of my car. The minute I saw the bike I slammed on the brakes, though after all those drinks I don't know how I found it, knowing that it would do no good. As soon as I stopped I jumped out to find the body, and I found it. It was sitting up in the road with no face. Sitting there like some macabre joke. I ran to the shattered bloodied body, the liquor still on my breath, and knelt before it and wept. Not because I was drunk. Not because only the back of the head was shattered, but because he was beautiful. His eyes so innocent. I knelt before him, gathered him in my arms, and wept.

The police didn't come for an hour, but when they got there I was still holding the child. They, the police, tried to take the body away from me, but I wouldn't let it go. I held the tiny body to my breast and wept, rocking back and forth. That was the longest night of my life.

The parents of the child didn't press charges. How could they? How could I? You can't press charges on yourself, though I wish I could have. Yes, the child was my two year old little boy. He was my one and only child, then and now, thirteen years later.

He was my baby boy.

The Disturbing Case of Joseph Luck

Part #1

Joseph Luck walked through the Sears store in San Francisco. He was following a power ring off of someone that he had been hired to locate. This search had almost been somewhat stimulating. He had almost broke a sweat, yet by the third day he had found the beacon. The individual that Seph had to find was a female law student that had skipped town in her parents BMW and a couple thousand in cash. She had also taken credit cards and even though the metaphysical was his calling, Seph had fallen by the way and had begun to take find jobs. He was the most talented agent in the field of parapsychology, yet that field was pathetically small. Most of the others that were even in arms reach couldn't do some of the things he could do. It was creepy sometimes. He could pinpoint someone within the state he was in sometimes, depending on human influence and occupation. He considered his powers as a type of telekinetics and spirituality. He could read thoughts of people in the street. He regularly had spirits and entities speak to him, whether he wanted it or not, and he sometimes had insomnia. The last was from his sped up metabolism. It was almost the same as a speed freaks, only he could eat and he occasionally got some sleep. Occasionally. Recently he had been having dreams, nightmares. They seemed to center around a demonic presence that wants his soul, and for someone he doesn't know he gives himself willingly.

He really hated to have dreams like that because every dream he had ever dreamt in his life had come to pass. Every dream. Kind of hard to ignore that kind of track record. Now most of the time the dreams were not so horrific. But for the last three weeks he had been having the same dream over and over and over.

He moved past the pants in the woman's section and felt her in the aisle to the left. He parted the Jordache and stepped through the rack to the other side and looked about himself. She was off to the left and hadn't seen him yet. He moved over to where she was browsing the teddy section. She had the fingers of her left hand slightly caressing the lace of a purple little number, and he entered her mind, her thoughts, and took her farther, therefore clouding her mind to him giving him the time he needed to get to her. He touched the back of her neck and placed her in a mind loop that would hold true the entire trip back to Seattle to her parents.

Three days later. He sits at his home just up from Cambria on the central coast. The Pines by the Sea's were south of his modest two bedroom cabin and the craggy shores of Big Sur were to the north. He enjoyed the verdant browns in the autumn and the sweet green of spring. His home was quiet and nature surrounded it. So why the hell was he so jumpy?

He had dropped off the girl to her parents, collected his fee, and been back within a twenty four hour period, and had not returned his offices calls. He was out of sorts for some reason and that reason's evasive quality disturbed him. The dreams had become more vivid and now involved the period after his enslavement to the demon where he resides in a hell like setting. He didn't really mind the enslavement, the loss of his soul, or even his time in hell. What bothered him was that there was no time setting, and the individual was still enshrouded. Those two things were always present, except in these dreams.

He sat on his porch for the bulk of the day, sunning himself and drinking Corona's with limes. His thoughts wandered and then coalesced on an energy coming towards his home. The feelings coalesced into a car on the road coming up the hill at speed. Seph began to smile as soon as it came into view and uttered one word in a mixture of reverence and disgust, but mostly humor.

"Daylatt."

The champagne colored Citroen spun out in a cloud of dust and the drivers' side door flew open. Out from the inside popped out the one person in this life even stranger then Seph. Daylatt Jones, white wasp metaphysical princess. Blonde hair piled on her head haphazardly, curls on end in some spots. The off white, no maybe it was eggshell. Anyway the tutu she had on was dirty below the waist. Also below the waist was where the cheetah spotted leotards and the combat boots. Above the waist was a chest that after two reductions still broke the thin back it was attached to. Over her chest was a leather jacket, lace strip through her hair, and huge rhinestone glasses. The really odd thing was that she was only twenty two, exactly half the age of Seph, yet she was ancient in ways that he could never be.

"Seph! Jesus Christ, this shit sucks!" She almost seemed to fly at him and stop right at his face her feet landing on the ground a beat behind the rest of her.

"What sucks, Daylatt."

"Those fucking dreams my dear." Her eyes were wide and glistened with the emotion she was feeling. It was what she called her curse. She was empathic. The most powerful empathic Seph had ever met.

"Yeah. Kinda a drag. I sleep better if I take short naps. I've branded sleep runes on myself. They help a little."

"You poor thing." Her hand reached up for his face and touched his jaw line. Her face moved up to his and they kissed.

He pulled back and smiled at her.

"I really need more talking right now."

"Right." She smiled at him and moved a little closer, "But don't think you'll escape me all night." He twitched a little as her fingers brushed his already lengthening penis.

"I don't think I could Daylatt. I don't think I could."

They had a nice dinner, and then they retired to the porch for the sunset. Seph had purposefully kept the conversation light for fear of some intangible thing. What it was he couldn't say. Hence the intangibility.

"So do I have to strip and begin fucking you before you talk to me?" Daylatt had a way of always getting to the point, sometimes by roads less traveled.

"No. Not yet at least. It's the dreams Day. I have them all the time now. They start almost before my eyes close, and then their in my minds eye when I rise sometimes as many as four hours after I lay down."

Daylatt sat and listened. Seph was leaning on the railing, His heads in shadow and yet his white hair shone like a beacon. After her suicide he had drawn her out of her depression, a feat that had seemed impossible mere hours before his arrival and consequent stay at the hospital. Her parents had died and she had not yet transferred to the state. She had been seventeen then.

"You see Day, It's not the dreams themselves. It's the fact that I can't pinpoint the time or the individual involved." They hadn't talked of anything related to his dreams yet, but she knew what was happening. She always had. "And it's not even that", he continued" necessarily. It's more the feelings that associate with the demon. I welcome it. I have absolutely no fear or avarice in what I've been shown. I sympathize with the demon's need for enslavement. That is what's unsettling. I don't really care about my soul."

Later. The sweat just cooling on their bodies, she disengages herself from him and moves to the window and lights a smoke.

Seph rolls over to the side facing her and pulls up the sheets.

Daylatt turns and her silhouette smiles." Your beautiful Joseph" She always called him Joseph after they made love. He liked that.

"As are you my darling. As are you."

He's before it and it's huge.

The beast rises above him almost to the height of a two story building. Its head is a cone on the elongated neck that smears out to a huge body wallowing out of the pit from where it crawled. The winds whipping out of the pit can easily be classified as gale force yet he remains on his feet. Certain brands are glowing on his body, protection, healing, grounding, strength. He hears a scream and he turns to his left....

The room is completely white and radiant. The woman, almost Angela Landsbury but not, stands in the center. Hands clasped before her she walks almost to him and stops five feet out from him.

"Hello." He said.

"Hello Joseph." it said.

"Is this it?" he said.

"Yes." She said.

"I choose to live then." He barely caught the look of surprise on its mask then the room was ripped away and the demon grabbed Daylatt. As it pulled itself back into the pit from where it came, Joseph through himself into the pit opening, using the brands placement and purpose to shield him from the closure's violence. Simultaneously he cut at the demons grasp on Daylatt.

The blade of thought moved from his elbow, encompassing the hand and jutting out to about three feet beyond the wrist. He formed it over his left hand while using his Right hand as a lever by increasing the power level in his fingers. By increasing the power he was able to force the crack wider. His left hand/blade slashes through the demon's tentacle and Daylatt dropped to the ground....

He woke up and reached for her. He felt her breathing and when she didn't answer his questions he lit the lamp. Her eyes where pupil less ands she was gone. What was her, what made her who she was was gone. She was consigned to the pit because of him.

The cabin sold later that week. No wonder when he marked it so low on the market. He turned the sale into profit for the journey ahead of him. A journey of a lifetime. A journey to find a soul.

The Shame

Manheilm adjusted his yarmulkes for the third time that hour. He was nervous. Very nervous. Someone somehow might find him out.

The child was crying and Manheilm thought, you're early. You must be cold. He took out the scalpel and began to make the incision on the boy. Now he stated wailing, so to complete the process Manheilm did the patented wrist curling to the left rotated cut that left the newborns foreskin neatly in the circumcision pan.

Later on, as the family thanked him again and again, he could think of one thing and one thing only. His home. Where it was.

In the car he could barely keep his knuckles from going white on the steering wheel in the anxiety driven grip he had on it. He was a horrible horrible man and worse, he felt he had fallen from his path and his responsibilities as a rabbi and a mohel. But he couldn't help himself. It was an affliction he could not repress.

When he reached the driveway he had to keep himself from running up the driveway. At the door he fumbled with his keys and he had problems unlocking the door.

Now inside he takes himself to the spare room, walking as slow as he can, savoring the moment. There in the room he opens the closet. There in the back room, in a quiet suburb in Ohio, a rabbi replaces his beloved yarmulkes for the black steepled top and wide brimmed lunacy of a witch's hat and feels ashamed.

ANYTHING

I look down the cliff face and wonder how it came to this. My love, gone. My child, the union of my seed and her fertile body, gone. Not to mention my sanity, even though I am more sane at this moment than at any other I will recount. I write now in this diary by the light of a hurricane lamp. I have a small and meager shelter by this high and treacherous place, yet not long ago I would have considered this place my most sacred sanctuary.

There had been a party that night oh so long ago, a huge ball to rival that of any held in this area in many a year. My wife, Caroline, had been so beautiful as well as my son. My young and innocent boy. Two beautiful people who were no more. They were lucky; at least I think they were lucky. They got two chances to live, yet the first life was more human than the other. The other I had made from sweat, blood, and the knowledge from the book. I apologize. I'm getting ahead of myself.

The ball had gone wonderfully. It was a gala that had only the finest food, the finest wines, and the finest music. Beautiful people dancing under the glittering chandeliers that hung from the open beamed roof in our central room. The evening ran late and when the last laughing guest had floated out the door it was well past three of the clock in the morning.

Caroline was walking away towards one of the two huge tables that were against the wall as I was shutting the door.

"Darling", she asked,"what's this?"

I crept up behind her and encircled my arms about her. I held her close to me and looked over her shoulder. She was looking down at a book.

"I didn't know you could read Latin, Dear."

Her question at that moment puzzled me because, dear reader, she knew I couldn't read Latin. But she could.

"I can't read Latin, my love." I said. "But look. It's not written in Latin, It's in the queens old English."

And that is the truth of it dear reader. It was written in some kind of reddish ink on an almost flesh colored cover. It was a huge and ancient looking tome and it was hideous. Dear reader of my now confessed sins, right then, right at that very moment I could have tossed that hateful thing from the very cliff that I now sit looking over. Could have thrown that despicable book out and over the edge and watched it plummet to the wave's far bellow. But I didn't and that is my curse to bear for eternity, but not for long now in this world.

As I stood there in the warm still hall of my forefathers she picked the book up. It came alive in her hands and began to writhe and then to fly open to some predetermined place within itself and came to rest. Once again the only sounds within the great hall were the fire crackling and the sudden exhalation of our breaths. Not until much later did I realize that there had been no gust of wind, no sudden draft of air that could account for the crazed thrashing of the book.

I almost wish she had dropped the book right then and there. Dropped it from our sight and kicked it into the fire to burn, if only I could truly convince myself it would burn. But the book became still, she held it and our eyes moved, almost as if they were creatures we could not control, up to the top of the text. I don't know what Caroline saw, and I thank whatever god that would listen that I don't, because she began to scream. It was a high pitched keening that went far above the normal human's vocal abilities. She slammed the book closed with all her strength and flung it from her.

The book flew, but altered its course to a table that was somehow behind us. We followed its unearthly flight and saw it land perfectly centered in the middle of the table and squared to all sides.

Caroline was still screaming. I turned to her and said her name several times, but it was to no avail. She didn't even see me. Her eyes were fixed on the book. I turned to look at it only when her cries became more strident to find the book open again. It was the same passage that it had revealed to us when she had held it. I turned to her and gently slapped her across the cheek. She stopped shrieking and looked at me with terrified eyes. Then her gaze slipped past me toward the ceiling and she collapsed in my arms.

I lowered her gently to the ground and made sure that she still displayed the signs of life. I checked her pulse and her breathing was regular, if not a bit increased. I stood up from her body and almost unknowingly found myself at the table containing the book. I was staring again at the open pages set before me by some unearthly gust of ethereal breeze. The words on the pages began to glow a phosphorous green. The color spread and engulfed my entire body. The last thing I remember was reaching out for the table.

I came too looking up at the concerned face of my son. His small little face with eyes that could swallow me whole.

"Father?" he said. "Are you all right, father?"

My smile quickly faded when I realized where I was. I was no longer at the table. I had fallen to the floor. The only thing I had managed to grab was the book. The fleeting thought that I should hurl the accursed thing from me came and went in a breath. The next thought was that my son would eventually take the tome of knowledge from me.

I moved to stand up and then remembered my wife.

"Son. Your mother, where is she?"

"She's upstairs and refuses to come out of her waiting room. I'm afraid dad"

I didn't wait for him to finish. I moved to the stairs and up them in the time it took for him to call up after me.

I found her in her antechamber staring into the mirror. For a moment I saw her with the only look I had never seen on her face before now. The look of a woman in extreme terror. She realized I was watching her and as she turned her face to look at me, it altered. The corners of her mouth became softer. Her eyes were calmer and clearer. It should have brought tears to my eyes to see her acting as bravely as she could for me, but it didn't. It only served to fuel my anger and hatred of her. An unreasoning hatred that blotted out all other thought and feeling till there was only room for one emotion.

I still clutched the book to my chest, and I honestly think that she didn't see it. In fact, I don't think she saw much of anything. She smiled the same vacuous smile at me as she had at the mirror. Then her head swiveled back to the mirror. Her expression never changed.

Before I began my work on the book, to crack its evil codes of rune and phonetics, I left explicit instructions as to the care of my newly made invalid wife. I hired the best doctor of neurological disorders and made up a guest room for him. I wanted him close to her, to be able to care for her. I wanted no interruptions from my work that I was about to begin. I hired nannies for my child for around the clock. I made sure a kitchen staff of more than the customary single serving girl and cook were there for any thing that anyone would want or need at any time they needed it. I did it all without looking towards the tower that contained the book. I made sure everything was in order before I ventured up for my first lesson in arcane knowledge.

Then I began.

It took several weeks before I could put together a comprehensive lab adequate for my needs. I first had to break down the book into sections. I comprised my first lists of page numbers and spell components needed for simple summoning spells that would allow me easier knowledge than simply reading every page of the arduous tome.

It took about a month.

As soon as I became more familiar with the different entities and spirits that were easily conjured I began more difficult summoning. I began to summon entities that I could bind to me with simple runes or strings of sounds that would do anything for me. Anything.

The book told of some of them, others I found by creating my own spells of a sort. Some of the more simplistic phonetics were easily changed to mean or do something totally different. I found the Succubus that way. I was reading by candlelight and found a strange off shoot string of complex vowels and consonants and pieced a string together. When she appeared in the circle I was not dismayed.

She was beautiful. She stood in the middle of the pentagram I had inscribed on the floor in the center of the tower. I had laid a three level circle to insure that whatever I was bringing to this world would not escape. The principle layer was blood from the slaughterhouse, the second was water from the ocean, and the third was rat intestines. The first layer was to bring her over, blood is an essential working for demon conjuring. The next layer bound her to the spot with the power of the oceans might. The last was a mystery I still cannot explain.

I said the chant and waited, and she came. She seemed to step out of a red mist that developed inside the circle and spread upwards to the apex of the ceiling. There she stood with the wall of blood behind her, legs spread slightly with her small and delicate fingers curled into fists on her bared hips.

"What is your name?" I asked her.

She tossed her red tresses in mock disdain and asked "What do you wish it to be?"

I didn't answer her for a moment. Her beauty was all encompassing and seemed to have me in some sort of thrall. I found it hard to look away from her nakedness. She was the perfect specimen of a woman and her beauty was entrancing. She was not beautiful in the way that my wife was, or had been, but in an evil all knowing way. When she saw me looking at her in lust, she began to smile. The smile sent a shiver down my back. The smile seemed to say to me that she could show me wonders of coupling that no human could perform or even dream of. Wonders whose payment would cost a man everything he had. Wonders that would cost a man his soul.

I paid that night and got everything that I wanted and more.

She began to come on her own after that first night and many nights afterward. I don't know if it was a weakening of some ethereal barrier or if my craving for her found her in hell and brought her to me. I began to lose my need for her when the work on the book commenced and after spurning her only once, she never returned. That first experience was my warning. It was a warning that I didn't or wouldn't hear.

The next conjuring was for a familiar to help me in more ways then purely carnally. I was interested in the flesh as any man, yet I was spurned for the true knowledge that the book could give me.

I began with the section of the book marked "Reptilius". It was there that I found the makings for a hideous demon from a frog like clan of netherworld dwellers. It called for freshly killed toads and frogs of several different sorts. I was almost a week waiting for the shipment from the town to arrive so I took some time from the book to see my family. Well, that's not entirely correct. The book allowed me to leave.

It was a strange period in that respect. At times I would forget to eat entirely and the knowledge would slow its steady beat against my brain of outpouring education long enough for me to realize that I was famished. It happened more times than I can fully recall. I feel now that I was merely a vessel for this almost sentient book. It was unnerving to be released from total consumption in a thing and realize your life is no longer yours.

I first went to my wife's doctor, after a bath and a shave. I had no idea how long I'd been in the tower, yet when I passed a mirror I was astonished to see my face covered by a full beard. My eyes were also full, with knowledge I thought. I passed one of the serving girls and asked her what the date was. When she told me I was shocked by her answer. I had been in the tower for four months.

When I saw Caroline's doctor it was painfully evident of two things. Caroline was no better then when last I'd seen her, and the doctor was frightened. Of what I'm not sure. He spoke vaguely of hearing strange things in the night outside in the courtyards.

"Have you seen anything?" I asked him one evening. It was the second day I had been down from the tower. We were having dinner outside and he had been on edge all night.

"Mostly just eyes. Glowing eyes. Alex, whatever you're into, I can help…."

"No actually you can't. I'm on the road of knowledge doctor. My education has exceeded your pathetic grasp of knowledge in the human body by leaps and bounds. It's positively frightening how involved you are in a medicine that presumably cures the sick yet you know not how the person becomes ill. I have learned the sicknesses and ills of the ethereal dimensions doctor, and I'm still learning. Knowledge is power doctor, but my power is greater than yours."

After that we ate in silence.

I went to see my son. He was larger than last I'd remembered, but his eyes were still so innocent. I was so proud of my son, my essence made flesh. He was a beautiful boy. What came after the resurrection was not, could not, be him except in the most superficial of reproduced features of face and body. Yet again I rush past the stories body to look at its tail. I apologize.

He was sitting on his verandah in the sunlight. The light was fading slowly down the patio and he was caught momentarily within its confines. He was an intelligent boy and as always he was reading a book. I've pondered repeatedly over what that book was. It escapes me now as it has on other occasions and the loss of the complete remembrance of that one shining moment in time rips at my very soul. The reason why dear reader is that that was the last time I saw him alive.

He seemed very sad, almost in a melancholy nostalgia. He looked up from the book held lightly by slender hands, surgeon's hands and his face brightened. The book dropped in the chair, forgotten, and he ran to me laughing aloud. As I saw him run towards me the light faded and the patio was lightened to a mellow orange yellow. I almost strained slightly to be able to see the sunset.

We talked in the usual semi-disjointed discussions that occur between adults and children. He tried so hard to be cheerful, yet it was killing me inside. I loved him so much, but I couldn't truly stay away from the book. My thirst for knowledge had overrun my life, and more importantly I was almost able to break from the book. I had lost the driving force behind the last months spent locked in the tower.

You see, dear reader, I was lying to myself. The true mastery of my soul still lay between the pages of that accursed book.

We had dinner out on the verandah. The night was cooler than normal for the time of year, but it was not unpleasant. The food and drink was exquisite, yet I couldn't free my mind from the book. It was beginning to take control of my every thought. It was an abhorrent yet pervasive thing. I would look at my son and realize that the underlying thoughts were of his use in a conjuration or spell. It was horrible. It was hideous. It was calling to me.

I could actually hear it in my head. The book was calling to me and I went to it. I went to it as a mindless driven thing. A thing no more in control of itself then a monster created by some mad doctor of the sciences.

The shipment came in towards the end of dinner and I oversaw the loading of my strange supplies into the base of the tower. I wondered if any of the delivery men could see the strange green glow that came from the top of the stairs. I was surprised when they went about their business of loading and unloading the truck.

After everything was completed I went to see my wife before I went up to the tower once again.

I entered her room and saw her lying back on her divan, an arm thrown over her face and the other over the side facing away from me. I came into the room and stopped in horror. Something vaguely reptilian was attached to her arm. It had a sucker appendage that was at the end of a long pointed skull. I went quickly to her side and pulled the hideous thing from her arm. At the end of the sucking mouth was a row of small pointed teeth. The creature had cut a small circle of flesh from her arm and had been steadily draining her. I crushed the creature under my heel and looked for the doctor. I found him moments later sprawled in the corner of the bedroom. He had a multitude of circular holes cut from his flesh and had been dead for some time.

I hurried back to my wife and saw that two more of the creatures were on her. One was on her neck and one was on her abdomen. I pulled the one off her stomach and then moved to the one at her throat. As I pulled I heard a wet squelch, the creature came off of her, and blood began to flow from the cut in her neck. I crushed the leechlike thing beneath my heel and grabbed a towel from her boudoir.

I ran back into her room and to her side. Her eyes had cleared and she was back from where she had been for so long. She turned her head and I could almost hear her neck creak with the loss of blood that would normally lubricate such a process. I glanced down and saw another of the creatures climbing her vanity table. It was absolutely horrifying. It was almost exactly like a leech, yet it had legs. Six of them. And the flesh of the thing had stretched taught and whitish with a reddish hue. The hue, of course was its body swollen with the blood of my wife.

I reached out and plucked it from the table, and crushed it. She watched it all with love in her maddened eyes. I could see she had lost control of whatever faculties she had left within her. As I searched the room for any more of the creatures I realized that her breathing was becoming slower and more labored. I went to her side and she looked up at me, and vomited what blood was left in her. I saw her trying to speak and realized that there was a thing in her mouth. I plucked it out and crushed it beneath my heel. She smiled and spoke to me for the last time.

"Where is our son? Is he safe? Is he safe??"

I told her I had no possible way of knowing and asked her if I should go to find him. She said yes, and released my hand she had been trying to hold. I left her side and went in search of my son.

I found him at the bottom of the stairs. His head had been crushed and pulped, and he laid in the entryway at the foot of the stairs in a steadily spreading pool of his own blood. When I turned him over his eyes were sunken pits of blood and gore. They had feasted on his eyes, and he had run to his death from the top of the stairs. I checked his wrist, but the pulse of life was gone. I carried him up the stairs to his mother's room and placed him on a small sofa, facing away from the rest of the room. As I wiped away the tears from my face I stopped at the door to my wife's room. She was dead. There was no possible way that she had survived. No living person is able to live with their skin stretched that taught over their bones.

After I wept for a time, I realized that I didn't have to lose my family. I could bring back my wife from beyond with the knowledge in the book. Now dear reader, remember my terribly agitated state and forgive if you can, for the further I go in the telling of this horrible tale, the less likely your ability to forgive.

As there were no more living beings in the home other then myself, I needed to procure a body. A living body, preferably a young one. The more innocent the better for these proceedings as the innocent before gaining the knowledge of the world have the power to withstand most things that would drive and adult mad or insane. That power was needed to bring about the horrendous act I was going to attempt.

I left them in her room and went down the steep hill to the town below. I had not been seen I the town for quite sometime so I was treated almost as a stranger. A stranger with an awful curse, and the primitive folk of that village knew it. As it was late in the evening, not many people were out of their doors, and most of them were drunks from the local bars, of which there were two. I could have used them for my purposes, but they would have been substandard. I needed the flesh of the young and the innocent.

As the adults wouldn't have worked neither would have the children from the whore houses. They had been used and abused for so long, their souls were ore lost and destroyed then the drunken fools outside. I had to take a child, an innocent, from one of the hovels that abounded the area. But not from inside the town, for then the cry would have been issued from every mouth and the story, as it were, would have been ended. That would have saved many of the townspeople. But I was not interrupted in my nefarious work and was allowed, through complete ignorance of my work, to continue it.

I found the small one room home out in the woods that surrounded the town. The family had been trying to work the land for quite sometime, it hadn't needed to be allowed to go fallow for quite some time, so they had probably only been working it for three seasons. Like a ghoul I crept up to the window and found them all asleep. The farmer, as is his want throughout time, is an early riser, and so at such a late hour was found recumbent in his bed. The small hovel had a separating curtain to give the illusion of two spaces within the small home. In one was the mother and father, in the other, the children.

I opened the door, and rushed to the bed of the adults and crushed their heads with the axe I had brought with me. Two quick downward strokes and their heads were split open and the pulp of their knowledge spewed from their heads and splattered the walls around them. I then was able to collect the children, after drugging them unconscious with a rag soaked in chloroform and placed them in a cart drawn with a horse. I took them back up to the house and carried them both into the room of my departed wife.

I did the deed in the room where she died. The power of her passing soul, and the lack of any use of it in arcane purposes allowed for a circle to be cast with real power. I retrieved the articles of power from the room atop the tower and the knives from the kitchen. I placed one of the children, the younger one, in the center of the room and began to cut into him, spreading out his entrails and bodily masses in the prescribed ritualistic manners described in the book. Any of the blood that happened to spill loose of the incantation seemed to draw itself to the book, some of it seeping into it at times. I did the chants and cast the spells, and the child's body began to singe and burn. To smolder almost. As the body's energy within its molecules began to be used up, she began to shake violently on the floor. The further along the body of the child got in desecration and immolation, the further her spasms and violent states increased. At the end she was suspended only on her heels and the back of her head, and then the charring stopped and her body slumped to the floor.

I crossed to her body and before I could touch her, her eyes opened. They were a different color then they had been in her previous life, and her skin was white, but seemed strong as hewn marble. She smiled and there was a small section of my psyche not yet totally under the currents of the book that recoiled in terror. She realized this, somehow, and the smile she shone at me was the most horrible thing I had ever seen. Then she seemed to soften, almost as if she were playing at acting, and began to weep. The tears were tears of blood, and her teeth were somehow sharpened. She looked unnatural and beastly and I almost drove a knife into her, but that wouldn't have worked. I didn't realize the extent I would have to go to to kill her a second time.

She rose into a sitting position, and gazed across the room with her yellow eyes. "Alex, why haven't you revived our son yet?"

"I'm going to darling; you were first and most precious to me." I answered her; fearful she would see the lies in my heart. But she smiled and walked slowly from the room.

I repeated the process with the same startling results as before and realized more fully the error of my ways. My son, or at least the thing that had taken the form of my son, couldn't even speak and shuffled like a beast. The head had somehow rudimentarily reconstituted itself, but it still looked lumpen and mismatched to the rest of the body. It shuffled out and was embraced by my "wife". I couldn't even touch the thing, it was no more my son then that thing embracing it was my wife. Even then I was trying to find a way, within my mind, of being able to destroy them.

As they parted from their unholy embrace, she glanced at me and smiled, and I shivered in fear. Her smile widened and she stated that her and her "child" was going to go to town for a while and to not wait for them. I was relieved when they left, but became more and more concerned when I began to hear the screams from the town and see the flames lick the night.

I went back to the book, that monstrous thing that taught and took with equal abandon, and searched for the way to kill them.

The town was in the act of ruination when I arrived. I had the axe again. The book had stated that only the separation of the heads of these creatures would end their preternatural existence. After I had scratched the ruins on the blade and had cast the spells of power over the item I was ready. Axe in hand, I roamed through hell.

The buildings were either burning or fallen over and destroyed. I searched for them through the town and came across all manner of pestilence, presumably brought about from the creatures I had spawned in my moment of weakness and loss.

One man was propped up in a chair against the wall of one of the bars. The top half of him was there in the chair, the other bottom half was nowhere to be seen.

A woman was writhing on the ground, a full mug of beer was in her vaginal opening and her screams were monstrous.

A small man, vibrating near me, upon sight exploded in a mist of blood. No matter survived. No bone, no meat, nothing remained of the man but a steadily dwindling mist that settled to the ground. Then crawled over and began to melt another dead body. I was unable to tell the gender of the other body.

I didn't understand how all this was possible from the abominations I had spawned, but I was prepared to destroy them the instant I saw them. I roamed for at least one turn of the clock and then found them. In some perverse twist of fate or luck they had stopped, possibly satiated, in the same house where I had taken the children mere hours before. She was stroking the head of the thing that had taken the form of my son, and he was feasting on the brains of the parents. Both their faces were covered in blood, as was their clothing. It looked as if they had bathed in the blood of the town. The entire populace must have been their sport.

I leaped through the door and brought the axe down on her arm, as she caressed the boy head, and buried the axe in his skull. She screamed and leaped back, taking her arm with her, as the axe sank into his skull. He began to make a gurgling noise and smoke from the wound that the axe had made, and wanting its destruction I had to leave it in until the total dissolution of the body had happened, I had no weapon to defend against her. And she knew it.

I turned and saw her place the severed bloodless limb back into its proper place and it stayed and began to function again. She hissed like an animal and leaped at me, trying to remove the axe from her small consorts head. I refused her intentions, and began to beat her back with a haft of a broken shovel I found in the hovel. Blow after blow rained down upon her, her face, her neck and arms, until I was exhausted and she didn't even stop in her attacks. She led with her teeth and bit through many sections of the handle, trying to reach me, but I fought her off with all the strength I had. In the end, it was luck and time.

Time because the child thing had fully deconstructed, and luck because of pure luck that smiles occasionally on the less fortunate and the unworthy.

I pulled the axe from the bed and the large charred piece in it and struck at her. I buried the axe in her shoulder, trying for her neck, and her head flopped over and with the force of the blow and the angle of our conflict, flew back into its proper place and trapped the axe in her body. Her smile was a mockery of all that that movement of lip and bone could convey. She grasped at the handle as if to wrench it from me. I used the force of our battle and the strength left in my body to throw her to the ground and wrench out the blade. I had to place my foot on her neck and pull with all my might, and it came free in a sickening wet sound. She turned off of her back and crouched against the ground on her hands and the balls of her feet. I swept the axe at her head again and she ducked my blow and leaped out of the window.

I ran to the window and saw her speeding out into the night, into the forest, running like an animal on all fours and howling. The few poor fools still alive that got into her way were cut down by her arms, twisted into hooked talons, and she then disappeared into the forest. I collapsed and my sight faded into nothingness.

Here I am again at the cliff face, staring down into the pounding destruction of the Atlantic Ocean and I ponder where my life has gone since the finding of that book. No. Not the finding but the acquisition of it. The *placement* of it in my life and the subsequent destruction of that life could send me over the edge into darkness and the blessed relief of oblivion. But I am not as weak as that. I need to find her, to follow her carnage and destruction and eventually find her.

I must seek and find my wife, and kill her for the sake of all mankind.

The Mask

I was barely 21 when I first saw the mask.

"It can show ya things!" said the one eyed man. "It can show ya visions!"

I didn't know exactly what to think. Here was this man, not very stable by the looks of him, asking me if I wanted to see visions.

"Visions?" I asked. "Visions of what sort?"

"Oh…..All kinds of things." And he turned away. He was suddenly like a man who had said too much. But too much of what I wondered?

I realize now that it was the wonder that cursed me from the beginning.

We were in a bar, a small strip joint really, in San Diego. But it really could have been anywhere. The red everywhere you looked was basically the same. Red lights, red tables, red booths and chairs. But the tablecloths were white, and for some reason it was those white tablecloths that caused me to cringe. Islands of sanity in a land of loud music and constant tired gyrations of women for shadowy men.

"So what about it? " I asked. "What about this mask? And what kind of visions do you see?"

The man wouldn't look at me for a moment. I could see the toil of the war between the need to tell, and the need for silence. He turned to look at me again and I got the real first look at him I'd gotten so far that evening.

He had white wispy hair that was thinning, an old mans face of crags and creases. But the odd things were his eyes. You could see them both blinking. One, the right one, was a piercing green of deep jade blinking the blink of consciousness and wakefulness. Yet the other, the right one, was trying to blink over the blackened hole that was the only evidence that he had ever had an eye in that socket. It was unnerving to watch. The thin flap of eyelid opening and closing over the hole that seemed to lead to the cavernous reaches of his inner cranial sanctum. Yet the clear, sane, still existing eye was the one that regarded me now.

"So ya wanna know the sight, eh' boy? Ya want the sight? Ya willin' to pay the price? The price is high boy, damned high."

"Yes."

"Think about it."

"Yes."

"Alright." He pushed his small weary body away from the bar, leaning heavily on the bar for a moment before pushing himself erect again, fished out a crumpled dollar bill from his front pocket, tucked it in the G-String of one of the dancers, and shuffled out of the door. I finished the last swallow of my drink, tipped the tired girl as well, and made my exit out of the door in his wake.

After the dim enclave we had quit ourselves from, the outside world was bright and glaring. After putting on my dark glasses and allowing my sight to adjust, I looked for my new found friend. He was standing a little way down the street on the right hand side. He was waiting, looking at me the whole time unmoving. We stared at each other for a few seconds and I followed him.

We, he and I, walked for a little. We talked, he and I, about small things together, the weather, the president of the time, other details that are used to fill the dead time and space between people that sometimes appears, unknown and usually, but not always, unwanted.

Finally, we arrived.

He stopped in front of an old brick building, gray with the smog and decay of the city and fished in his pockets for his keys.

"Where…fuck…." He finally found them and inserted them, still somewhat grudgingly, into the lock. It was a deadbolt, so I heard the familiar double click, and then the door was swinging in and we were entering.

The house, I have to say, was even odder then the man that owned it. It was two stories and more than likely was beautiful at the time of its construction and a pleasant place to live in. In its time it had probably been owned by a family, a nice "flowered wallpaper in the kitchen" kind of family. A nice "HisNHers matching bathroom towel set" kind of family. They probably even had bunk beds for the kiddies. That had changed drastically in the intervening years.

Something had come to the house. Something that had taken hold, probably not at first, and had ripped the foundations of sensibility out from under that little family, and in essence the house as well. It was not evident on the outside of the house, but the inside was a different story all together.

The top of the wall, the plumb line of it, had skewed to the left and down slightly. The stairs where the old man was now leading me had straightened completely out and then had accordioned back into themselves, and then had drifted back a bit to the right. The strange thing was that there were no cracks in the walls. The cracks that were there were from age only. It's like the house melted and re-solidified in the wrong dimensions.

The old man must have noticed the look on my face. He smiled slightly, and nodded to himself.

"You see? You see what the visions can do? I wasn't careful the first time. The first time ….the first time the price was much too high. Much, much, much too high." He sighed, and wearily started back up the stairs.

As I watched his retreating back I finally realized something. I didn't even know his name.

As I followed his slightly stooped back, I realized that he must know, or at least must have known, great power. I was almost near the top of the stairs, but I stopped short, suddenly wondering, was all this worth it?

The old man stopped also, and turned to me, quizzically.

I found myself asking him questions, inquiring I told myself. But deep inside I knew. I was stalling for time. I was stalling out of fear.

"What was the price? What was worth the visions and trying to survive in the aftermath?"

He looked at me, as if for the first time, and then told me.

"My family. It cost me my family, my job, and my eye. But all that comes later. After you see it, you'll ask questions. Then I'll answer. But not now. Not before you see."

He turned and walked down the hall where the stairs had ended therefore forcing me to follow, or leave.

I chose the first course of action and forever set my life to the task of following the mask. Following the mask till I found it, or I died trying.

* * * * * * *

I sat and looked at the leather mask and wondered why I was here. Up till now it had felt like a dream. No, an anticipation of a dream.

The old man had led me down the hall to the last door on the left. By now it was dark, but the walls practically glowed here. I didn't have time to wonder on the odd sort of light because the man opened the door.

Inside the room was a pedestal. On the pedestal was the mask.

My breath caught in my throat as I looked at it. The power and pain in this object could not be denied.

It was leather. The right side was drawn down in a rippling effect that looked as if it was trying to simulate a melting or dripping motion. There was no eye hole on that side. The left side of it had a perfectly normal eye hole. There was a zipper on the bottom of the neck that extended upward to the base of the mouth area. The area around the mouth was designated by eight holes punched out in a diamond like formation.

I realized the old man was watching me. I turned to him, and my breath caught in my throat.

His right eye was gone. The left was a sparkling blue and completely unblemished.

"You've used it, haven't you old man?"

"Yes." He answered quietly.

"How often?"

"Only twice. After the third time its not good."

"What do you mean 'not good'?"

He smiled slightly. A smile that was not friendly, caring, or even vaguely humorous.

"It'll steal your soul, boy. It'll steal your fucking soul."

* * * * * * * * *

I think back now and remember the fear at all this. The revulsion. And yet deep inside me the need. The feeling of need was suppressed within me, yet brought to the forefront of my thoughts. I wonder even now, all these years later, if this feeling may have occurred later on in my life. Possibly the second time. I was in my thirties…….

* * * * * * * * *

…and had been searching for the mask since that first fatal day with the old man.

After he had told me the penalties of a third time wearing of the mask I had fled home.

After a month, I'm almost positive, I had had such an intense longing to see the mask that I had returned to the old mans house. It was empty. It was secured with police tape. I looked around for anyone on the street, saw no one, and broke into the house. On first entering the house I was walking carefully, like a thief. When I hit the last door on the left, where the mask had been, I was sprinting like a lover.

I hit the door hard, not bothering to use the door knob, and slipped. I fell to my knees and looked up.

The mask was gone.

I cradled my face in my hands and wept.

* * * * * * * * * *

The second time was different. Much different.

I had, after the first time I saw it, begun research on the mask. I had tracked it to around the 1700's and had possibly found leads to it in other more distant times. The key was the person who owned it and the rarely witnessed showing of its power. The warping and chaos unleashed in the using of the mask and the power it used was incredible but oddly enough it was seldom, if ever, documented. The thing was, people seemed to shun the knowledge of things not quite normal or right. When I first heard of this, in the beginning months of my research, I was disgusted. Some of the stories were so monstrous if not totally disastrous. Now, after research and experience, I realize that the power of this thing, the absolute and total power of it, could shape people to its will. You see, it makes you need it. Even after the two times, even after the startling and disturbing visions and sensations, you want it again. You want it again, and again, and again.

I have cases, documented cases, of things unreal and unnatural.

Harold Garner. A husband, a cartoonist for an obscure paper called the Clarion, a father of twins, boy and a girl, somehow acquired the mask.

After the loss of his sanity, his eye, and his two vision grace period, he used the mask the third and final time. In the skewed aftermath of the house what the police found was astonishing.

The wife had mutated. Her arms were where her legs had been and her legs were where her arms had been, her eyes were in her stomach. The twins were worse. They were skinned, probably alive, and partially eaten. Mostly their pre-pubescent genitalia and their eyes. Gardner was definitely in better shape. The only thing wrong with him, or rather, exploded off of him, was his head. There was no blood found anywhere near the body. There was no head found near the body either.

The mask was never found.

In all the cases the mask wasn't found at the scene, but there was always an altar to it. A place of almost sacred reverie, where it had sat, had to have sat, and bled its power out of itself. Bled and waited. Bled and waited.

The second time. Let's talk about that for awhile.

I was, as I stated before, in my thirties and had been researching this thing that had taken control of me. It was almost…no, definitely perverse. A perverse need that shook me to the core. I began to realize I could sense it when I neared the thing. I had yet to even put it on, however. Though I won't lie to you, dear reader of my vanities and secrets, I wanted to. I wanted to wear it, probably for the same reason as everyone else that came in contact with it. I wanted, needed, to see. I needed to feel. I needed the mask.

I had tracked it, the mask, all over the world and had finally found it in Alabama. It was in a pawnshop, shoved in the back amid the old home video game dinosaurs and rusty knives. It was hidden from view and the proprietor, a young man vaguely feminine, possibly gay, found it for me. I had found it here almost by scent, so I was not perturbed when he had trouble finding it. He was muttering quietly while rummaging in the piles of discarded broken down memories when he found it. It was the same. I almost wept when I saw it.

"How much?" I asked.

I'm glad I had sense enough to hide my true feelings of total awe of the mask from him, for he looked me over before he spoke.

"Give it to ya for…..75 bucks." He said, looking for information in my eyes.

Needless to say, I was elated to have found it, the mask, that I would have paid almost any price for it. But I had to act indifferent for him, or suffer the penalty of pointed questions.

“I’ll give you 50 dollars for the…for it.” I said, praying for an end to this façade. I wanted to leave and use the mask finally.

“All right.” He said, and walked to the front of the store, to the tired pre-world war one register, and began to ring up a fifty dollar sale. He had the mask, of course, so I had no other course of action but to follow. So follow I did.

“Been here long?” he asked. I noticed the slight nasal twang to his speech that marked him an Alabamian. I wanted to be gone from here as soon as possible, but he looked like he wanted an answer, so I had to continue the game a little longer.

“Not long at all.”

“What brings ya here?” He asked.

My heart stopped for a full three seconds, then continued to work itself at pumping my lifesblood through my body and keeping my mind, the center of the visions, revolving around and around.

“I’m just traveling around, seeing the states. You know how it is.” I had started sweating slightly. I could feel a small drop running down the slight crevasse that my spine makes in my back. I wanted out.

“Well”, I said,” better go. Thank you again. See ya.” And I left, practically running out the door.

I paused outside, swaying slightly. I could feel the power coming off the mask in the small stained paper bag in my right hand. I needed to use it NOW. I was practically shaking, my willpower almost smashing down inside my mind.

Then suddenly, as if a switch had been thrown, I felt fine again. Tired and sweaty, but better.

I had found it, and survived.

But that was just the beginning.

* * * * * * * * * *

The forest I found (not a hard thing to do in Alabama) was deliciously cool. The leaves of the expanding canopy of trees took most of the heat and transferred it into a cool green haze. It was nearing sunset, and I had gone far from the trapping of civilization. So as not to disturb, disrupt, or destroy anything, and also to keep my find to myself. I opened my overnight bag, which I had brought with me from home, and drew out the worn, yet powerful, leather mask.

I could feel the power coming off of it in waves. Throbbing with an almost sickening intensity. Crashing and receding, crashing and receding, rocking into my mind with waves of power. It was calling me to enter this thing of visions and see where it took me. I grasped the opening into it with both hands. The inner side was smooth and unbroken. It seemed almost a separate piece from the outer section of the mask. As I began to don the thing, I could smell warmth and cinnamon and some other spice, not yet sickening in intensity, but a shade more and it would have been. I slipped it over the top of my head, the bottom of it passed over my eyes, I saw briefly from the holes where the mouth area would be, and then I felt it close over my head. The only sight was through the left eye hole and for some reason it had a rose hue to it. I wasn't sure what to expect, for the moment nothing happened and I was slightly relieved. The constant need and searching for the thing was bad enough, but the anticipation of pain and hallucinations was worse. Then I realized. I had yet to fasten the thing to my head with the zipper in the front.

I reached up and tugged slightly on the zipper. A small gasp escaped my mouth as a sharp pain hit my right eye. As it did a bright flash hit my mind and I saw….something. What it was I wasn't sure, but I was intrigued. Now I know it makes no sense dear reader, but you know I can speak only truths now. I was ready for the pain. I even wanted the pain, especially if it brought me those visions, visions of what I didn't even know.

My left hand shaking, I reached up and put it over my right, and I counted to three. One…..two…..on three I yanked with all my might, and blacked out.

* * * * * * * * * *

When I came to I noticed the wind first. On my face. Unobstructed breaths from my mouth. The mask was gone, or at least not on my face any longer. For all I knew the fauna of this area had stolen up to me in my delirium and had removed it to be spirited off somewhere beyond. I lifted my hands and felt something sticky and tacky on the right side of my face. I opened my eyes and realized that I was seeing in mono. My eyes. Oh god, I had done it.

The remembrances flooded into my brain of what I had done. I was appalled. I had mutilated myself for the gaining of information, visions, whatever it would give, and I came to the realization that *I didn't remember any of it.* I was as lost as I was before I donned the damnable thing and now I was missing my right eye. I reached up and felt the cavity that remained after my journey, and I began to weep. But only from the single orb that now stared wildly from my face.

* * * * * * * * * * *

It's now twenty or more years since that day in the woods. I have worked to amass a fortune and have done quite well in the intervening years. My home is purposeful in its design and opulent in taste, but I honestly don't realize it even when I'm here in it. I thirst only for the thing that gutted my eye and gave me something which I only get tastes of in dreams. All my dreams are haunted now, haunted and strangely disturbing. Yet when I awake I see nothing, I remember nothing. It all fades like gossamer spiders threads. Yet I'm not giving up.

I've been cruising the streets recently, and I have a plan. It's a good plan, as plans go, and I think I've found the man to help me carry it out. I could have chosen a woman of course; they haunt all the areas of any nondescript ghetto center of any large metropolitan area. Their eyes sunken and yet yielding. We all hunger, but they wear their hunger on their faces for all to see. Some want that in a casual mating, yet I've been beyond the act of coitus for quite some time. My urges are more terrifying, and the women recognize that before they ever get into my car. The men though. Their so much more malleable. For a meal, or even a bottle, they'll cross the great expanse and come into my vehicle for the long ride back to the house. But they don't have the stamina I need, not at first. So I convince them to stay, to gain their strength. The means of convincing are not important, it's the reason. You see, I won't go insane, I won't allow my urges to wreck my home, my things. No. I've got a plan you see, a plan to get all my visions with none of the pain and torment. My house is on a great parcel of land, and when their ready, I will take these small men with no lives and I will give them greatness and worth. At least in the final moments of their lives. I will force the mask onto them, and record their visions for myself. I have a bunker, at least a mile from where I'll restrain them and force the mask on, and I'll record it all. The screams, the visions, the ecstasy. I'll get it all and I won't harm a thing.

I've had the mask for years now, and the urge to wear it is at times over powering. But I've held off from doing it. I've remained strong and pure in my intentions. Tonight, you see, I have another one. He's strong and virile. He's got resilience within his body that I don't even think he realizes he has. But he will tonight. As soon as I have him restrained and ready, and after the drugs I laced his bottle with wear off, for I've gotten good at the correct dosage after so many times, I'll put it on him. And I'll pull the sipper down, and I'll run to the bunker, where the tapes and film are already going, and I'll watch, and I'll wait, and I'll see. I understand now what it takes to be a ma of vision. It takes the use of the little ones in the world. Why else are they there for me to use?

I have to go now. I have a plan.

In the Still of the Night

The sun dies in the west. The last embers are crushed by the darks sweeping emergence on the planets face. Night has come again.

Greetings. My name is Greg Stilson. My friends in high school (how long ago that seems!) used to call me stilts. I'm 79 years old and am a retired physics professor. I worked at Harvard University and enjoyed my work immensely. The kids were wonderful and my colleagues were tolerable. That's what I was, now let me tell you what I wanted to be.

I always wanted to be a frontiers man. You know what I mean. The kind of man that tracks the animals instead of killing them. But now, due to science and the beer breweries I've become too old too quickly. So instead of running around the countryside hunting for animal droppings I've decided to content my wilderness urgings with evenings on the back porch under the stars, listening to the animals rustle in the underbrush.

Oh, I'm sorry. Did I forget to tell you about the alternate dimension?

You see, my cottage is in the country. I mean the COUNTRY. We're talking a "lions and tigers and bears oh my" kind of thing.

Now the thing is that I only assume there is an alternate dimension. You see, I'm not sure. I can only surmise that the dimension theory is correct, even though I haven't seen a great yawning abyss, or seen a great tear in the fabric of space and time. Not yet.

I can only tell you one thing. I can tell you about the things I've seen.

After I started seeing things in the underbrush, I got a new companion. It's my father's double barrel shotgun.

It all started about a week ago. I had been retired now about a week and I had remembered this cabin. I had bought it from a man who had disappeared the day I had bought it from him. I think I know where he went.

You see, being a professor, I had researched my cabin and had found it to be a very interesting experience.

It was built in 1924 by a lumberjack. It was built, to my knowledge, by hand and has not been altered since its original erection.

The mans name was Gregory Stiltison.

My surprise was surpassed when after finding out the name of the man was finding out that he had, in fact, disappeared a week after the final completion of the house.

Now you might be thinking that he might have simply left. Or possibly taken a walk and have fallen in an old mineshaft. But I know he didn't. The thing is that when I bought the house and moved in, the next day I found tracks leading from the back porch into the house to a table. On it were two words.

Come home.

That was yesterday. Let's start back a little further to the beginning of the week. I bought the house on Monday. I had to stay in the city for at least a week so I could settle my affairs. As Friday rolls around I got a call from the sheriff's station. They said that the man that I had bought the house from had disappeared earlier that day. It seemed that no one had heard or seen from him that day. When the sheriff had gone up to the house to investigate he had found the house empty. Everything had been packed and stored in the attic.

The sheriff asked if I would answer a few questions. I said yes, answered them, then we said goodbye.

So Monday of the following week I find myself in the cabin. Everything in the attic is unpacked and set in place and I watch the sunset, while drinking a beer, and go to sleep.

Then the tracks.

On Wednesday, after cleaning off the footprints, I asked the sheriff if he would like to come up to the house so I could ask him a few questions. He laughed and said sure. He came over, had a beer, and started talking.

He said he had only seen the owner I had bought the house from once or twice, briefly, before his disappearance. He said that right before the mans disappearance he had seemed different.

"Different how?" I asked.

"Well son," he said, "different like he was more alive than your normal average everyday guy."

"More alive?"

"Yeah. Like he was electrified. Like he wanted to leave."

Like he wanted to leave.

I know what that man had to go through. And what it was like to have an access to another world. A world unexplored, unknown, untamed. A world with new and exciting places to discover.

Home.

You see, I know because, genetically, it's in me, I can feel it pulsing and beating in my body. I honestly feel younger. And I'm also looking younger. When I came here I was a 79 year old retiree.

There's no more grey in my hair. That left about Wednesday, I think.

Now then, the things in the forest. I'm not sure what they are. Some are huge hulking things; others are low to the ground. I don't know what they look like exactly, but I know that some are hungry.

I have a new wound that's mostly scar tissue. That happened overnight. Literally overnight.

One of those things got up close to me last night. It sort of reared up on a kind of tail. Sort of like a snake, but it was hairy. Anyways, it rears up and I feel a warm line trace itself diagonally from my stomach to my right shoulder blade. Needless to say, I grabbed the shotgun in about three seconds and blew the thing away.

It flew about five yards and hit the ground. I heard the underbrush start to rustle and I got back in the house. I didn't want to find out what fed on the thing I had just blasted away.

I went into the house and put peroxide on the cut. It was fairly deep, but was clean. Then I went to sleep.

In the morning it was healed. Nothing to show for it but a light scar that was gone entirely by late afternoon. I went outside, but the thing was gone. I could not find anything but some yellowy foul smelling pus like liquid on the ground. I didn't want to try tracking it. Not yet anyways.

I'm writing this all down because I want to set the record straight. Nothing has taken me away. I'm leaving on my own free will. You see, in one week I've practically de-aged. I'd now guess my physical age to be in my early thirties. My prime.

I've set all my affairs straight. I've gotten my sturdy clothes on and provisions for about a week. I figure after he left he must have built another house over there.

I've packed everything in the attic and have sold the cabin. You see, I'm going home. Maybe ill see the new owner there in a week or so, maybe not. Not all of us can cross over there. The reason I took time to write all of this was because when I started it was light out. I'm just waiting for the sunset, and the still of the night. It's about 7:30 now. As I look out the window I can see the darkness settling over the earth. They come to our world mostly at night, you see. So I think I can probably cross to their world at night also.

I've got to go now.

I've got to go home.

Poetry

DEATH

no

wait

i'm not done yet

NEWBORNS

What is it about newborns,

That makes almost everybody,

Flip their collective lids?

Let's be honest.

They can't cook banquets in your honor.

They can't write contemporary novels about our times.

They can't drive a car; they can't even reach the pedals.

They can't fly mercy missions over hostile areas for relief purposes.

They can't free political prisoners of oppressive regimes.

They can't clean the house, or even build one for that matter.

They can't be airborne rangers or combat ready veterans.

So why is it that their so damn cute?

I love newborns.

HOME

A legion of dogs,

Swimming the carpeted floors,

For a slice of your approval.

Mom and Pop,

TV tray of jalapeno's,

Five gallon cornucopia to be precise,

Slammin' 'em down,

To the tempo of a chargers game.

Off to my room,

Not necessarily a haven,

But the walls are mine.

Covered in retro Maidenesc,

Dancing starchild,

Groovin' to the beat of Devo.

Ahhhhh.

Youth.

ON THE STREET

On a street,
In any town,
In any time,
In any country,
Two people move,
Toward one another.

Each walks by,
Pretty shops filled,
With glass trinkets,
Others with knives,
The cutlery gleams,
In the anywhere sun.

They near the place,
both walking with,
Heads bent against,
The anywhere breeze,

And collide.

He looks at her,
And she looks at him.

That's all it takes.

SANDY QUAG

So there I was,

Walking in the dunes,

Oceano to be precise,

Miles and miles,

Into the "Fray",

So to speak.

So I'm walking,

With a dude,

I had not seen since,

…….

Well, since I don't know when.

So We're walking,

Walking in the dunes,

It seems like miles,

The sky is overcast,

And slightly grayish in color.

The dunes meld almost,

Without flaw with,

The sky.

Depth perception is absolutely screwed,

You seem to bump,
Continuously with the dunes,
Leading into sandy,
Soul kisses.

They're immense,
These sandy monoliths.
They seem to whisper,
Over and over,
That the true measure,
Of infinite space,
Is the key to understanding,
Ones place in the,
Scheme of things.

"Pass the bowl!"

Inhale the true sight,
The herb of great,
And monstrous,
Visual acuity.
Hangin' at the top,
The sandy mogul,

The silicone giant,

Sits silently,

Whispering,

Calling.

Exhale.

“Quag!!!!”

PARTIAL DYSLEXIA

I saw a sign which read

"Beware of God", and thought,

Should I be?

TiMe

TiMe tAkEs uS AlL,

SoMeDaY EvEn i wIlL,

hAvE To gO.

A ship.
Flying through space,
With the most special of cargoes.
Human life, animal life, plant life.
All in wait (stasis) for the end,
Of their cosmic journey.
The journey to rebuild,
To rebuild all that was lost.

After we destroyed,
All but 7% of the world,
We built the ship,
In the remnants of humanity,
And launched her, with crew,
Into the outer vacuum,
In hopes that she, ship and crew,
Would find a way to restart,
Us, and not our mistakes.

She's in the cold and waiting.
She can wait forever.

WHY IS IT?

why is it,

that people,

everydayer's like you and I,

have problems,

giving of themselves to the ones they love?

why is it,

that life,

that supposed precious,

and finite aspect,

fraught with the most,

perilous and trying of times,

be so infinitely painful?

why is it,

that people consider,

only the aspects,

of their own meager,

existence instead of,

the totality of their own species?

why then,
when love is,
professed to the,
supposed keeper of,
said individuals heart,
said individual uses cruel and punishing implements(words)?

why is it,
that people seem,
(the every day,
normal shmoe,
you understand)
so unabashedly keen,
to bolster their own,
happiness and understanding,
by totally destroying someone else's?

why is it,
that they do,
this in ways,
not even conscious,
yet harmful to,

themselves and others of their own species?

Why is that,

Do you think?

Road

The regrets of doom ladened ladies,

Brings trepidation to ghostly boys,

Adieu.

And when, heavy brows dangling,

Ghosty boys retire,subduued and chaste,

Rising, things and stuff continue to diddy-mao.

The moon casts a baleful eye,

It's ocular beam lances,

Yet falls short the mark,

It's light is diffused.

A child, nay a man,

The fur on his cheeks,

Not yet ripe for scything,

Moves through this light,

With somewhat measured trepidation,

Through heavily forested evergreen,

That rolls ever onward,

Over hills, through valleys,

And tries to claim back,

It's independence from humanity.

He moves through to the edge of the forest,

A clearing is presented.

Wind stills,

Hush descends.

Nature waits for the victim's first step.

The victim obliges.

At center he stops.
Nature and the victim wait for death to come.

Death obliges.

It moves on two feet with feral cunning,
It's bloodlust flows through every fiber,
Freezing the victim,
Rooting him to absence.

It comes to him,
An embrace of blood,
An embrace of death.

It tears open,
Its lips are wetted,
By the flow of innocence,
That gushes in red ribbon,
From the neck of youth.
It satiates upon the flesh.

As the rush of heat,

Given as sacrament to the beast,

Cools in the night,

Death howls out its lust,

For all things living.

Back arched in reverence,

To the mother moon that transforms,

It vanishes into the forest,

To continue the hunt.

WHY THE BLOOD AND GUTS?

Why do I crave the horror genre?

Why do I hunt for "Fangoria" at the Barnes and Nobles bookstore?

Why do I leap from my seat, acting ass snake bit, when the heads start to roll?

Why do I find their F/X so fascinating?

Why, during Romero's "Dawn", do I move closer to the screen during the human gut fest?

Why do I wonder if chicken parts were used?

Why does real death and suffering in agony hurt me so?

Why aren't I desensitized yet?

Travels

Field Trip #2

October 26th. At about 6:15 P.M. I left my house to begin the odyssey to the PG&E building. But not for any "Diablo is good for everyone and everything" kind of propaganda. Oh no. I was going to get closer and "get real" as they say with....E.coli. So I left the 101 freeway at Higuera and drove the long way to the center. The PG&E center is located on the frontage road that faces the freeway and has a tri level parking area. The lack of real night time lighting made me wonder if I had screwed up and missed the night. After a slight nervous cringe in the abdominal muscles, and after I had climbed the steps up to the door, I realized it was open and this was the night. The first person I saw was Mr. Ruppert, cruising the area, mingling and shmoozing. I asked him directly, and another gentlemen as well for handouts, but none were available. So then I waited. And waited...And waited.

First it was where to plug in the laptop. For some reason the projector was unable to be sized to the correct size for the presentation and there was much switching and plugging and resizing verily I say unto you. Then the batteries went out, and there was much running about and gnashing of teeth. Then the gentleman that brought the laptop, who turned out to be a man by the name of Donald Weston, begins the long trip to presentationland.

When I had entered the room, at the beginning of the night, I had sat down and begun to write out my notes. My actual notes, because of the lack of handouts, will be presented at the end of this typed paper. So, as they began to fiddle with the laptop, and there was a lot of fiddling, I wandered out of the room to where the coffee was. I noticed along the walls allot of different awards and such thanking the generosity and loveliness of the company that is PG&E. I made it to the coffee {and by coffee I mean sugar and creamer and caffeine..} and began to make myself an elixir of caffeine. There were young girls there as well, and after instructing them on the ways to a perfectly round physique {like mine} I returned yet again to the room.

Still fiddling. The phrase"ya want me to get out my projector?" comes from the front of the room. The idea doesn't really go far until Weston switches it. The projector is switched in the middle of another guy trying to fix it, and he makes a grunt as if struck. He makes the sounds of "I almost had it!" The original projector is replaced, some slight grumblings, and then the fiddling continues. And continues, and continues.

The corners of the room seem to coalesce into groups of people that know each other. I'm loving that my choice of the back of the room allows for a certain lack of interference and an over all viewpoint that allows for better information gathering.

People begin to gather and the seats fill up a bit more. The teacher that substituted for O'Neill enters the room and is absorbed into the group at the far left front of the room. Approximately 20 people so far showed up. More fiddling occurs with the laptop and the projector is switched. Things settle somewhat and the meeting begins with Ruppert and his wonderful world of all things biological!

First he begins with the member totals. The biological society has approximately 89 members; up 2 from last year and the year before was 3. Their

20th year was that meeting {I think}; a member had lung cancer and was thankful that some of the members had visited him. The society is led and controlled by a group of people, which seemed to be all of them there that were regular members, called a steering committee. The steering committee allows for not just one person, or even a group of officers, to control the biological society, but anyone that chooses to attend the steering committee will be heard and allowed to decide the direction that the biological society will go in. And there will be no lovin on the E.coli this evening.

The first talk was entitled "Tracking the sources and causes of toxicity in an agriculture affected creek." Boy, was it DRY.

Originally the aquatic life of the fish was being destroyed and this caused the study to be done. The main study was about the toxicity levels in one particular creek, bordered by Hwy 33 and a series of drainage ditches within the Salinas valley in a high risk area. Originally the use of organo-phosphate pesticides, which were derived from gas attacking agents in the wars, caused massive problems in humans so they were discontinued and pyreethroids were then primarily used by farmers and also in large suburban tract home areas. It also seems that if one should encounter a pesticide with a "thin" end to it, that is a pyreethroid based pesticide. Within the substrata of companies employing these chemicals, 123 companies were involved along with 608 products. So the state of California decided to do a little research to see if possible removal from production would be needed, and had this team of scientists head out and take samples in a seriously problematic area.

The tests are basically that the scientists take a certain fresh water shrimp and place it in a sediment solution, because the pyreethroids attach to the sediments and bond with them, and then at the end of a 10 day period, the live shrimp are counted and the amount that die off from the original 100 is the percentage of pyree's in the culture at the time, or the toxic levels.

The tests showed that from the west to east markers along this small stream the toxic levels didn't actually appear till the drainage ditches were reached. To give an idea of the levels, from the mountains till the drainage ditches were levels of toxicity of 2 to 7, but when the ditches joined the stream it jumped to 100% till the San Joaquin river was reached on the other side of Salinas.

They then proved the existence of pyreethroids because of a temperature difference test where if the temperature is raised or lowered just 5 degrees the shrimp either live or die in greater abundance.

So, after massive slides and other intrusions into my brain by scientists, I came to the conclusion that pyreethroids were bad for fish, but the worse cause seemed to be unreported spraying of these chemical substances within the agricultural areas around the ditches, but the worse contributors would be the people living in their homes spraying out the bugs like there's no tomorrow. The toxicity levels in the poor creeks by the suburban areas were even worse then the agricultural areas. Primarily it's because of the turf builder products and the sick needs for a better lawn, and raid and those products as well.

So, as my poor addled brain leaked from my ears, yet another long winded and stammering scientist comes to the front of the room. Her name is Charlene Ng and she begins to describe the ways and means by which they got the core samples. I must say at this point the term "yawn" doesn't do the night justice. I found all the information informative and fascinating, but the constant bombardment of the words "pyreethroids" and "Hyalella Azteca", which was the name of the shrimp they used, kind of hard to get. At least from the layman's point of view.

So, I learned that once again man as specie is killing off all those cute little creatures in our quest for a better lawn and a more perfect head of lettuce. Oh. I have to go spray the carpet with bug killer like the wife wants.

Raggorama

I've got the Hawaiian shirt on and I'm in the bathroom when I hear the wife say "take this to your father please" to the little monkey girl of my world. She troops up the stairs, not unlike a ..er..trooper, and she hands the phone to me. It's my buddy calling from a payphone to tell me that the bus split without him. Fairly cheesy is my auto response and he agrees. I'm thinking that this will be a short night out fer me if we never get started so I tell him I'll come pick him up and we're on the way.

So after massive kisses to all the family and my love is known and acknowledged I'm off once again to see a band that I've had shoulder brushings with for about 10 years or more. Ragg. The only band I've ever heard that did a punk style rendition of somewhere over the rainbow. And I tell ya readerlings..it was a tasty angle on that tune.

On the road I went to an outlet mall center near where my buddy was ditched by the bus system in our area. For some reason, at least according to said buddy, the bus systems drivers had all left for their real jobs within the public school systems driving the big yellow busses and the public transportation system in the area needed to get some folks in fast for driving. Since that has yet to happen, buddy at a payphone at 7pm at night. I cruised by the store where he was at, talking to a friend he hadn't seen in a long time, and he hopped in the car and we were off. I had one of those bizzarro malt liquor energy things and we shared it on the way with massive bowls smoked to the herb gods.

We hit the parking garage, the self same parking garage where the last time we saw a band at the same place we were going to to see Ragg we were not only hassled but also chastised for smoking some herb by a parking attendant that was I think MUCH younger then I. He said things like"I expect it from these young kids (tried not to laugh at that one) but I figured you guys were smarter." Now I don't know about you but when I get lectured by people about the intelligence of smoking herb versus drinking and destroying my liver I want to ask them if they thought George Washington was stupid. Or Thomas Jefferson, or Benjamin Franklin, or any of the founding fathers not to mention all the music and art and literature that was and is a direct result of heavy drug use and debauchery. The one thing that supremely irks me out is an uneducated public that believes the propaganda that their own government uses to dumb them down. So, we parked there again, and when the heights where climbed in our minds, off we set for the bar and Raggs performance.

They were playing with two other bands for a cover charge of two dollars only, so not only a good time but affordable as well. I had a fifteen dollar certificate for the specific bar we were going to so I laid it on them and got three rum and cokes for my troubles. I gave one to my compadre and I inhaled the two others and the party was officially started.

The first groups name was machine and they were actually pretty good. When doing the bar band circuit as a spectator you never know what your going to get unless you know the band already. All things considered I was pleasantly surprised by machine. The songs were rockin and the lead singers' pipes were nice and limber. Since my brain refuses , unless repeatedly abused, to remember names of people I have no clue whose in the band called machine, but they was good. Then Ragg hit the stage. The guy and girl that basically are the driving force behind the band and its music greeted us warmly and so we hung out with them during machines stint. Then me and my buddy hung out and watched Ragg shred the stage from their little booth they had staked as their own.

Now the last time we, same buddy and I, saw Ragg they were in a different incarnation called Catharsis and they shredded. They had a girl singer, as they did in Ragg as well, and she looked like she was twelve. Both my buddy and I looked at each other and in unison asked the same question wondering if she was old enough to actually get into the bar or not. Then she opened her mouth and the demon she was hiding inside of her came out. It was a mind blowing experience to feel the music crashing over you as you witness a force of nature unleashed. It was a truly awesome show. And like all their shows, Ragg was not a disappointment in any way shape or form. The singer they had this night was not too impressive until she started to sing, and then like always (why I question them at all is truly beyond me) I was blown away. So blown away I actually bought 4 shirts, got TONS of stickers (which I have a tradition of sticking, if the band rocks, to the outside of my computer case and they are there of course. I'm installing it now!) and their EP type thing with a few songs on it. So, shirt for son, daughter, wifeykins, and I done I left to go to the car to drop off the shirts and things and to get a little more change in my head and then we were back into the mix. There was the 3 or 4 college kids rockin out in a 4 person mosh pit of their own designing and others huddled back from the lights of the stage in the darkness, nursing their respective alcohol libations. As the waves of sound began people would leave, but not as many as this small town should have leave, maybe they knew what was in store and were here to rock as well. There was never more then 30 to 40 people in the bar, counting the bands I might add, at one time which is sad judging the music that more people were not able to get into and onto it.

After the Ragg rocked and rolled we, same said buddy and I, hung out with the band and I made sure they were all "taken care of" if ya know what I mean. After their set I helped them load their truck with their equipment and got to see the "backstage" area of the bar we were at. Kinda cool when you help out and then are considered a part of the band. I always seem to be able to do that; at least if I know them and they know me. While we were lifting and loading there was a situation for the guitarist of Ragg and a set of keys. While trying to find them the bouncer door duder and I went back over to the booth where we, the band and my buddy and I, were at and he whipped out a 200 dollar flashlight. After the shock faded slightly I was able to form the cohesive question on the mind of anyone involved with a person that has spent 200 dollars on a flashlight. "Dude…what?" I have to admit that the flashlight was incredibly bitchin, but not 200 dollars worth of bitchin.

The band parked the truck over near the backstage area and as I loaded a bowl, the guy in the car next to us started talking to us. Found out he was the canvas for a show called battle of the tattoo artists or something, a show on lifetime I think he said, and he had what looked like an iron on patch on his lower left back. It was a tiger shark and the art was incredible. Then he took off his shirt and the whole underwater theme came to the forefront. He had manta ray; the tiger shark had the moray fish skimming along on it, and some other fish as well. Truly amazing art and needless to say the artist that worked on his back won the contest.

The other lead guitarist had lost her leather jacket and I helped in recovery of said item, a bizarre trait I've had for years, and kinda tripped her mind out a bit. The trait for some reason simply allows me to find things, usually that people had been missing for some time. I've been led to hats on hillsides that have sat there for a week's time, bowl lids off of friends' pipes that are on the floors of friends' houses, little things that are sought, but evasive. Afterwards we headed back over to the bar front door where the bassist of Ragg was hangin out. This guy looked like a young Bill Nighy to the T. It was a wonder that no one else had ever told him he looked like the actor, I was his first and was proud of it. So I made sure his head had lifted slightly off his shoulders, and me and my friend left to head back to his house. After dropping him off at his house I headed back to my home, to while the night away playing with my website and grooving on the net. Till next time ….Adieu

From the Ridge to Vermont

One Hippies Jaunt from the Western Edge into the North Eastern Kingdom and Back Again

This tale could easily begin from the date I started the odyssey from the western edge of the Americas into the center and out the other side, but it begins before that. It starts on a hot day in Paso Robles California. The wifeykins and I were heading to Wally world to get something for her friend who was graduating from the nursing program that's been taught here on the central coast for years. My own sister is an alumnus and I was happy for my wife's friend so we were trying to find something neat and since Wally world was on the way, we went there. The wifey, I, our daughter and our son, as a club or group, headed into the store and I heard.."(My name here)! "And I turned towards the smallish yet fit woman and realized she was in my creative writing class in college and I knew both her and her hubby. We had lost contact with them a few years back and since then they had propagated into a small yet mischievous girl child and a cute and EXTREMELY friendly boy. I said hi and her son did the 7 month old leeeaaannnn towards me, so being horrendously addicted to children I grabbed him automatically and then held him for the entire "in store" visit we had for that day. Her mom was with her and we were able to meet her, we exchanged numbers and went on our way once again in "damn we're late and need to shop quick" mode.

Now let me tell you dear readers, the parting from these folks was weird weird weird. We had gone camping with them at a really neat yet fairly obscure camping site up where we live. One of those down a country road into the nothingness kinda place, but it was beautiful country. Lots of bizarre and strange granite formations and the sere California countryside poking through from time to time. There's an unbelievable cold stream running through a rock area right near the campsites and my beautiful wifeykins, when she went in pregnant with my now 7 year old child, got the "damn this is cold" look on her face and my child , in utero by the way, pushed out of her skin away from the water. My wifeykins ended up moving out and just dangling her feet in the cold cold water. So, me and the dude head up into the hills, almost to where we could walk over the hills and see Big Sur spread out underneath us, but we didn't make it. I had frozen a steak and put it in my backpack for the hike. As I was starving and ready to rest, the walk being uphill for the entire way, I found an interesting rock formation that formed almost a natural chimney so I put it to good use in cooking my steak. The wind was blowing pretty hard that day, but this chimney structure was really light of wind until it hit about halfway up the structure. It was formed of a couple slabs of what looked like the red rock that's scattered all about the sandy hills out where we are near the coast, and then it went to the left slightly about seven to eight feet up. Then it continued up about another five or six feet and tapered off into the sky. So I realized, being a black belt in pyromania and a Californian and psychotic about wild fires, I made sure the fire was low enough and not too "sparky" because I realized if the fire got out of hand at all I was hosed penally, and we were hosed physically. A fire up there would have out ran us, and consumed us and the rest of the area. But I kept it under control with little or no effort, but the paranoia from hubby ma was insane. He never, through the at least 45 minutes cooking time, stopped considering, loudly, the chances of conflagration, nay the certainty, of conflagration. Constantly. It was trying but I figured that once I got the fire going and cooking, I could just get him loaded and we'd be better off all around. I had brought booze, but I hadn't really been alone and out of familiar surroundings before with just him so I figured, cannabis is fine but booze would be a mistake. So I cooked the meat, then shared with him, thank the goddess that his appetite wasn't harmed in the cooking of said steak, and we continued until we had to return to the small area we had chosen for our sleepy time spot. Had its own fire circle and everything, but since it was high fire season we didn't want to have a fire that close in to the albeit small population. So we climbed to the almost top, where the sand dunes we were obviously climbing began to taper off down slightly, but before the view, and we headed back to our little spot and passed out. The next day we left back down off the hills to our original campsite with our wifey's and went to the unbelievable cold stream for a dip. Afterwards we got to the drinking, my poor wife was preggers so she couldn't even drink a thing, but the rest of us ended up almost killing a 3.75 liter jug of I think Captain Morgan's. As we imbibed the sun was going down and the other campers were starting up their parties so we decided to travel a bit. We left our campsite and walked over to a much more open camp site near the front of the campground proper. As we got closer to their campfire area we noticed that the tree we got to leading into the campsite area had at least three throwing axes, a couple regular camp axes, some throwing daggers, and a couple ninja starts imbedded in it, which for this little tree huggin hippy its more then a little painful to see. So there we were, walking up to the fire and we see the folks hangin out around it.

They were mostly agricultural students from Cal Poly San Luis Obispo and were all and all good natured. Then the weirdness increased about a thousand fold as the hubby starts to make lewd advances towards these guys women. One of their women was naturally bronzed skinned and was a beautiful woman, and he starts in with the "Are you an island girl? Ya know what they call them?..Huh? Huh? LBFM's..Ya know what that is??" and so on and so forth. His wife, my friend from English class, says something about hating a sweatshirt she's wearing and throws it in the fire. I was surprised we weren't asked to leave right off, and there were a few tense times of course, yet they calmed down a bit and everything got calmer. Then when we went back to the campsite, he drops his pants and tries, unsuccessfully, to get his wife to perform fellatio in front of us. So after I got him to hike his shorts back up and they went into their tent, my wife and I were treated to the sounds of bizarre sex and her saying that her bladder hurt and she felt like she was going to puke. So as she's puking out the tent flap, naked, he's mounting her from behind. For every thrust of vomit out he would push back a bit. I have to say that reliving this year later in my head is still icky and yucky, yet I can't stop the pictures. So I got down to her level, she was on all fours, and I covered her up and got him off her a bit, then I gave her water because she was so dehydrated. After we got back to their house and we watched the husband try to attack another set of friends on tape, my wife and I distanced ourselves from them. We hung out after that time for a bit, and they did get to see my daughter, but all in all we were done with that relationship.

Until now.

So now, its now. The numbers were exchanged and they ended up calling us to come hang out at her parent's house and we acquiesce. We had a barbeque, and he was as weird and bizarre as ever, but it seemed the birth of two children had mellowed her out a bit, and made her make him more adult and reserved. And I have to admit that their children were extremely well behaved and well mannered, which being such a rules and manner policeman is a beautiful thing to behold. Their daughter definitely has the eyes of a mischievous little monkey though, and she had a real "three stooges fan" kind of humor. So in all ways, a connoisseur of high class humor. And of course during this fated visit/bar-be-que was where the question was raised that would later take me across the United States and into web site writing oblivion. "so dude", he says" (her sisters name) was thinking of going back to Vermont with me when I fly (his wife's name) and her mom and the kids back to Vermont so you wanna go?" In my head was the automatic "WHAT" kind of thing. I'm thinking "golly. You mean spend like WEEKS in the car with ya and have no where to go." But what came out of my mouth was "Well duder, I'll check with the wifeykins but I don't see how I can afford it." To which he replies "Well hell man, all you need is a way home and I'll take care of everything else." To which I replied "We'll see man." And we left it for then and had some severe foodalicious and hung out with her family.

And that was it for quite some time, though I did have a conversation with my wife that went something like this.

“So hun, check this out, doofus asked me to go to Vermont with him. Crazy huh?”

“Why don’t you go?”

A beat then, “O.K. Who are you and what have you done with my wife?”

“No really, you won’t get a chance like this any time soon, so why don’t ya do it?”

A beat then, “ok really. Who are you and what have you done with my wife?”

I get the look, the eternal look that through time and space has gone from every wife to every husband when said husbands jokes and ribbing become tenuously tolerable if that and its now time for him to shut the hell up. So I moved on to the next point.

“How can we afford it? I’m gonna have to have money for the trip and all. And I have no idea how much this will cost to get back home.”

But in the end she convinced me and so I began about a two week search of all forms of travel from the great state of Vermont and in particular, the great north eastern kingdom. And I found out how incredibly convoluted it is for a traveler to travel who doesn’t ever not drive somewhere in his own car. First I hit the airlines, and that was a sobering experience for a person like me of constant limited means. Then I checked the train system and found that in some instances it even more expensive to go on the train versus flying through the air. Then I checked the bus, the hound, and it was absolutely the right price. For only 126 dollars I was able, over three days and 11 hours, to make it back from the northeastern kingdom to the west coast of California. Since that seemed to be the best deal, I went for it. I mean hell; the bus ride would be gnarly, but doable. So the plans were set, and the wait was on until the day arrived and he showed up on my doorstep.

We hopped in the car they had rented I guess to get around town while they were here. I guess they were at her parents, where the bar-b-que had been, and had been parked there for two months solid. For some reason they had just sat there at her parents house without leaving for two whole months and were wondering why they were going crazy. Any child at their parent's house for two months above the age of about 13 years old I'd be guessing would have an issue with it. Its not that the parents were bad people, no ones parents are bad people, they were just the parents. It's the law of the jungle or something. Anyway, the whole plan was that we had to get to Saratoga California to a campground they had found on the internet, so we had a bit to go till take off time in the R.V. They had to get the rental car they had back to the agency from whence it came, so we took it back and came back to the parents joint to ready the Bega, what I ended up naming the R.V even though, as I was told repeatedly by him, it was a Conquest! Later it became known, as far as the rumors and the legends tell, as the man cave. I vote man cave myself.

After going through stuff that was outside, and tanks of toilets were dumped, and other water tanks were filled, children were loaded on the Bega, mothers, daughters, and sons came aboard and we were gone. The trip had begun at last.

I had come prepared for a trip. I had about a half to three quarters of an ounce on me, and a wood pipe to not trip the sensors for metal usage. I had brought with me a copy of the album Orb, Orbs Adventures Through the Ultraverse which is a truly amazing record, along with the album Them by King Diamond, Oxygene by Jean Michel Jarre, some Dead Kennedy's, The Essential Fishbone by of course Fishbone, Deep Breakfast by Ray Lynch, and I think 2nu This is Ponderous which is kind of a new aged thing with interesting tunes along with a monologist feel to it, a storytelling angle one might say. I tried for a fairly eclectic cross section of tunes for the road. After this trip though, I really wanted to get a MP3 player or something. I'm not one for ipods to be honest, neat toy but way too much money when for less I can get more bang for my buck and not have to convert every music file I burn from CD into an ipod friendly format. I like my music at MP3 levels. I figured for the cruise up there I'd break out the Orb and let their kids groove on it. I know my child loves music in general and she dug the tunes from the universe of Orb so I let loose on them. And they loved it. The kids, at least their three year old daughter, started to car dance before she caught herself, and the adults were grooving to it as well.

The ride was pretty much uneventful, though there was a bit of a psychotic angle when they though they had gone too far and had yet to reach the campground. But a few miles later the campground rolled into view and he actually proved his ability at parking the Bega. He backed it up directly and professionally into the space right by the stream, so we had that pleasant sound trickling all the time at the back of the Bega. Then he cooked dinner.

Now I'm the kind of camper that cooks over an open flame, preferably if I'm able I choose to catch the food as well. Trout has many times made it onto a spit over fires I have made in the deep dark woods, so to see him crank on the propane, after popping out the sides of the "living room on wheels", and then meticulously cut, into each things separate bowl, items for the stir fry. I bailed out the back as her mother hung out with the three year old daughter over at the playground that was there, and she fed her son breast milk and smoked a little herb to my head. About five hours in a Bega with two small kids, a family I'm not a member of, and the respective mother in law/mother was kind of an experiment all on its own. So it was with great relish that I, as the dormouse said, fed my head. I tried to write a bit but the sun was failing me, dying in the sky as I tried desperately to chronicle my time, so I gave up in hopes for more time the next day. So I gave up and went in for dinner, which was very good.

That night I couldn't sleep at all, even though the knowledge of a 5am wake up call was burning constantly in the back of my brain. So I walked around, snuck hits here and there, and cruised the half filled park in the moonlight checking things out. It was the first time I was able to truly be alone and wander with my thoughts through the park and think. Think about the drive, so far and further on, and to experience the place I was in. I had made a pact with myself that I would try like hell to get into the spirit of the road and the spirit of the trip and not preconceive constantly. I was trying to throw out all the crap in my head about him, or her, or the mother, or even myself. I wanted to capture as much as possible the feelings and experiences I had, and would continue to have, on this trip. I wanted to be the conduit that I had never truly been before. Staying true I guess to the form of it, the trip the writing, and not slacking off or giving up on it. It was one of the few times that I had created for myself an attainable goal that through procrastination or simple sloth I would not be able to slight or slack on.

In the campground was this bridge. I guess the bridge was over the campground, but the part I explored was the structure of it. I've never taken any architecture classes but I've always been attracted to it. The style and little idiosyncrasies of it always thrill me down deep so I give into it. While in Germany in Frankfurt I found an alcove between three buildings where there were little stone monkeys hanging out of the wall and swinging off of other little monkeys. Little pockets rarely noticed or seen. So I was originally looking for a date, after the relative concealing nature allowed for head feeding I was looking for, to tell me when the thing had been built. It being night ad pretty dark, and since I was being a little sneaky and sorta ninja, I was sparing with the flashlight so I didn't find it, but I was impressed by the structure and the feeling of it. I sat underneath it and wondered who had gone across it, who had jumped from it to take their own lives, who had proposed to a significant other on it, who had gotten their first exploratory love beneath its granite arch. What stories did it have to tell?

So I climbed around the bridge for a bit, checking out this, nosing into that, not breaking into anything, just checking it all out, and then I went to where there were tents set up. I think they were for either a day camp thing for kids, or they were set up for a bar type salon thing they had going there. Underneath the leg of one of these covers was a purple SkipBo card that was the number three. Being in the frame of mind I was in, I wrote in the book I carried in the back pocket of my shorts, and still do, this cryptic scrawl: "Skip Bo #3, purple found under leg of 'pavilion' type white tent. Meanings in the dark?"

{Next Entry}

Tues. 7/10/07
Near Sac Town/Cali
8:21 A.M.

Word of the day is obstinate.

Dropped off the women folk at San Joser airport at the skyjet Armada with much hugging and child control. As soon as they left we went to an area where he could switch into his "hippy" clothes and settle in for the journey.

So, kidless, a few bowls (woody ones) into the day for this intrepid informer and a hit or two for him. Massive map checking endured and patience exacted till the "80" magically appears. Slight personal vindication flows into bizarre behavior from him. For now,
Adieu.

9:20 same day

NPR faze. Strange freaky avoidance of Wal-Mart. Convo goes..

"Dude. There goes Wal-Mart number four." Says I, pointing.

"Oh wow. Dude, I like, Can't get over." Says He, pointing.

Not a secret that I need to go to Wal-Mart. Have been asking for awhile now. Strange power trips.

Adieu.

{continued}

Questions forming. Grasping hands at the notebook I'm writing in. Power strangeness from him.

{10:48 A.M.}

All Vermont and no play makes Jack a dull boy.

Adieu.

Non-Adieu.

Closed eyes for a bit. Allowing for quick mental reload. He uses his puter, banking and other items. Chess site allows now to check percentage of players moves went which way, when decoding a move in response to opponent.

Italian salami used in snacking by him seems to produce copious and uncomfortable gas. Getting the weird side aches.

I keep drifting. This sleep deprivation thing blows. Wish I had a valium. Slept lots day before travel. Checking.

Got something small and blue. Think the ride back should be mellow. Or at least I should be well rested. Might have slight residuals that could be augmented by cannabis.

I can see the act of this “experiment” in respect to my writing is in and of itself a singular and unique experience.

I can see a different self emerging. I’m seeking the calm place between moments. Questions, interference, even the prospect that this would or will go anywhere, all of it mute. Malleable. Muteable. I see no true destination, only the journey. Or at least I’m trying to. Is this my wilderness? Is there a grail to be sought? Or did I leave my Grail behind? My relationship to my wife, kids, daughter, son, and further into distant genealogical times? That’s the Grail for me. The culmination of all my life, all information. All of it, passed into my lore, my rock. I so dearly love them.

Adieu.

7/11/07

6:28 P.M.

Left Sierraville hot springs.

He’s a freak. Spent most of yesterday and today naked in various forms carousing in tubs filled with hot water from natural springs. And sand generously applied to the floors of them. Headed first to the meditation pool. Met a girl and a guy, both nice. Told us of the festival that went down last night. Too bad we missed it. Hippies and music and all the trimmings. Sounded tasty, but oh well. The reason I know about her is that she talks incessantly about herself, then shows me flyers pertaining to her career in music, T.V., and festivals. She vindicates herself with her singing later on in the communal music area in the "compound".

The rain has met us again. It came to visit last night. He had set up the camp, let out the awning, and (with wishful thinking) had set out about five chairs, two tables, and was slinging the Chivas. As the chilling commenced, the sky began to tumble off of the back of the mountain in front of us. As I thanked the higher being for helping me remember my duster, and she said welcome, I donned my duster armor and walked toward the storm. Now this was after MANY (two) shots of Chivas. I walked towards the storm, I believe laughing maniacally, and found after many tufts of sage, pines soaring up to the ionosphere and rotted wood I found a perfectly circular patch of dirt and sat, as they say in pre-school, criss cross applesauce. Still laughing.

Later I learned that she of the musical voice was in the pools as the storm raged. When I learned I was jealous. Pools in that tumultuous storm would have been amazing. Being absorbed into the pools warmth while the skies raged would have been truly spectacular.

So I crouched for only a short time, approximately five to ten minutes, then rose to head back to the Bega/Conquest. To be honest, it was fear. Fear with awe at the forces unleashed on the mountain ahead of me and the air above and to the side of me. At one point I was certain that lightning had cracked the air to sizzling currents directly above me.

Got back to the Bega/Conquest, soaking and smiling. He, through all of the magnificence, stayed shuttered within the Bega/Conquest. Opening the window, leaning outside an imperceptible inch and spoke with his lips to the opening. Every time I entered the Bega/Conquest a gust of tornado strength peaks would enemize the Bega/Conquests interior.

Back to the now. He's repeating himself over and over "hippy chicks" and other sophomoric sexualities. Has now reverted to "mouth" fart noises. Already four hours on the road and he's looking for a space for the RV. He has no real driving stamina.

Nevada. Seared, yet some vistas at first, in the distance, of greenery.

At less then a quarter of a tank he decides to forgo gas and head into the desert in search of hot springs. We're headed back, taking the 400, a little used highway that eventually leads into dirt.

Adieu.

10:51 P.M.

Battle Mountain, Nevada

7/11/07

"Looking" for hot springs. Gave up on Kyle hot springs, couldn't/wouldn't find it. Had less then a quarter tank of gas and split back to 80 East. Got gas-"Lets head father man." "We couldn't find it." Great, he's still including me into the plans that don't work. And I'm not included into the plans. Not allowed knowledge or forethought.

10:57 P.M.

Now off the 80 East. “Looking for crescent valley.” He tells me. An old Indian women told him.

Adieu.

1:45 A.M.

Elko, Nevada

Morning of 12th

At Wal-Mart parking lot. Surrounded by other RV’s. First Wal-Mart stop since Mondays request.

Carrot or Mule?

Cart or Horse?

Dangle and Flop.

Next morning

We head into the Wal-Mart here to get a new laptop for duder. He left his on the table of the RV as we were in motion and wonder of wonders it falls and smashes. I didn’t say anything because his reticence to listen to any ideas or thoughts is pathological. So he gets the new puter, freaks out and begins to spaz because it doesn’t work and refuses to uplink to the internet. As the tension mounts I install the headphones, newly purchased, into my ears and watch on the sly. He spazzes, he smashes, he roughly crams the puter into the box and takes it back after lots of grief on the phone with tech support. High tension because he can't check his site.

7:26 P.M.

Wasatch Mountain Range, Utah

Up in one of the canyons that abound about Salt Lake City. Air conditioning running, side's popped out. Roughing it.

Things seem to be calming somewhat. We tried to get into a hot spring here, but were not able to. They had a class in there for the rest of the day and we're not hanging for another day. He's done meandering and wants to continue now at a decent pace. Went over to the locals spot and soaked in a hot hot hot spring right out in an area surrounded by mansions and houses. Other people show up and we hang out a bit, then travel back to the campsite. We take a walk together, chuff off a cigar a bit, but resume the love of cannabis. We walk around the campsite and head back to the RV. I call a friend in the area but she has no wheels so can't get to where we are. He's not into driving to her, can't really blame him, so we hang and chat.

9:29 A.M.

7/13/07

Lyman, Wyoming

Listening to Fishbone as we cruise across Wyoming. Mello semi-normal chatty Kathy night. Past mile marker 56 in the big Wyom. Rolling hills with weird fences built probably to somewhat lessen the degree of the winds power.

Past highway 30 to Pocatello. Quick smile from the usually Idaho bound boy, myself.

Strange plateau's, lonely sorta, more melancholy then anything else. The distance is what's staggering. It's the unnerving almost mountain but really it's just a plateau. Strange.

11:25 A.M.

Near Rawlins, Wyoming

Odd billboards abound the I 80. Supposedly the Rockies are where we're rolling through, but it has a distinctive Wyoming like appearance.

He continues through the entire trip to be cell phone intensive.

The geography seems old, tired imitations of the stretch of the 101 in California where the seared brown "plop" of dirt and scorched vegetation reaches down from a couple hundred feet down to the sea.

At truck stops, so the flashing sign tells me, they have savings accounts. I find that odd for some reason. I understand the reasoning, truckers and all, yet.."GET GAS! START A SAVINGS ACCOUNT!". Little strange

11:56 A.M.

Finally, mountains. Finally cooler as well. Mugginess is gone from the air. Still plateau's, yet they rise, one, two, three, marching up finally into the space reserved for birds, planes, and possibly deities.

Strange clouds, strange because it's weather, actual weather. Cloud formations instead of freaky wispy things. Actual…oh, we're by it now.

Massive amounts of trucks travel this road. The smells are light, almost cilantro in flavor in the back of the throat. Sagey smell, delicious.

Real honest to god mountains rising into the distance, snow still on them. Not sheets, not blankets, not tempurpedic, but more ribbons really. Air is sweet. Actually sweet. Different then in California. Sweeter, higher taste.

The unnerving thing is the lack of trees. Real trees. Serious scrubland thing, with an occasional tree or two interrupting the plainness and the sagebrush.

Wyoming does seem to have the wind generation thing going. Just cruised by the second batch of them. Seems to be about twenty or thirty of them and their all turning. Too bad the field in southern California can't let go their need for oil.

Seeing rain streaking from the clouds ahead. I truly think the term "expanse" had yet, at least in my own head, to be truly explored or delved into. Wyoming allows for that I think. Little of the curving phenomenon I witnessed in Montana with the wifeykins.

I miss my family. I miss them terribly.

Rain seems to have missed us at least for the moment.

Thick clouds shade the road in strips, light, dark, then light again. Can't stop smiling, it's beautiful. Cows grazing in a line heading east. Rolling plateaus with mountains or at least some semblance of peaks.

Rain! Scattered reflections on the glass.

As we head further east clouds are darker.

Adieu.

7/18/07

7:38 P.M.

Kirby Vermont

So we made it. Did some hard driving. On the day of the last entry we drove over 900 miles. Started from Wasatch state park in Utah and that was the last park we stayed in from that point on. So, from the Wasatch to 90 miles from Des Moines, Iowa.

From that point we cruised through Iowa, Indiana, and stopped for a truly amazing steak sandwich in Chicago.

Was a place called "The Big Chill". Thought at first it was an ice cream shop. It was, but they also had other food items. Ravioli, steak sandwiches, sausage sandwiches, kind of a hole in the wall delicatessen place. Guy that owned the joint was way cool. He had learned how to cook the items in his shop from his mother, who then over time had gotten Alzheimer's. Most of the conversation up to that point had been jovial, but he was, understandably, upset mostly with the difficulty not only emotionally but financially trying to help his mother. I asked him in all honesty why he didn't head to Canada for the meds, and he looked what I thought was hesitant. But it was not truly the meds that upset him, but the fact that his mother, the woman that kissed his wounds as a child and taught him his vocation was one day soon, if not already, not going to recognize him.

From Joliet and our melancholy yet jovial friend, we made our way almost to the border of Canada before we stopped at a rest stop again for of all things, rest.

Side note-In Iowa at the "Prairie Meadows" we, he really, played the ponies. Twenty dollars became one hundred and forty four (twenty included) and a buffet later we were on the road. The number bet on was number three, taken from the skip-bo card I had found and chronicled.

Now the colorful group there with us was the real show. Egging on their horses they had bet on by yelling at the televised races on the screens before them set up around the room. It was on the upper most floor and a little woman, about four and a half to five feet high explained the basics and he won, after we figured it out. Lots of forms and weird mathematical yearning are involved in horse betting. As we were waiting for the race we had betted on to begin there were quite a few races already going. A man, his age because of possible teeth loss and soft consonant sounds, was difficult to determine. An African American fellow with rhythm in his voice was yelling at the screen that had totally absorbed his attention, "whip 'em sum!" and "Get 'im off da rail!" and other unheard horse race incentives shouted at the televisions across the united states betting parlors.

So, after a good snooze in Michigan we headed across the Canadian border and made our way onward to Vermont.

Side note- the funcle uncle. Between Utah and Iowa (Eye a way! As they refer to it on the music man) we stopped at his uncles house in Colorado.

When we drove into the "gated community" thang I totally felt like I was suddenly thrust into a John Hughes film. All of the houses, including his uncles, were what I've come to designate "John Hughes Midwestern".

Now all the way there the build up to the uncles, by him was saying things like "He's ultra-conservative". I had on a tye-dye, of course, and he says "You have any conservative T-shirts?" All this silliness and wouldn't ya know it, was all an act. Uncle became in my eyes a very cool duderoo. Gave us "America to Fascism" by a guy named Russo I think. Insanely good and I watched it all. All about the United States governments need to screw not only the rest of the world, but of course its own people as well. Excellent movie. As we left I noticed a sticker that looked like a gay pride rainbow flag. The funcle uncle as in truly phunky was told, and his eye got a little scared, and got worse as I told him of my pride that my seven year old daughter has gone five years running to gay pride in our area. So then it was off to the road.

Through this trip it's been a constantly a test. I know when I ride the bus the test will crest. Hmmmm. Poet and didn't know it thing.

Adieu.

11:55 P.M.

7/18/07

Kirby, Vermont

Sitting eating strawberry rhubarb pie from the giant apple place in Canada. Yummy. Sitting in the RV, where I've been living the high life, having pie and studiously writing away. Just got my ass kicked by his brother in the game Risk.

It's been a few quiet days since we arrived. Was approximately 2am on the 16th of July. About two hours out from the United States as we cruised was hectic. But let's remember Canada.

We crossed into Canada, I'm sure smoking a bowl, seemed to keep his weirdness down. So we roll up to Canada, smiles blazing, my tye-dye (brought a few) glowing with an almost preternatural light.

12:51 A.M.

7/19/07

Kirby, Vermont

Just talked to the wifeykins. Daughter lost a tooth, son gained two teeth, and our cat died. Called my daughter, she's sad, but with the cousins and giggling. She wants another cat. Can't blame her.

2:53 P.M.

7/19/07

Kirby, Vermont

And made it through. “Where’s Los Osos?” “What’s your occupation?” I love it when I tell people “I’m Mr. Mom!” And it seems to be different between geographical, cultural, and gender lines. The guy at the border, my Canada cherry popper some would say, his eyes widen, leans back a bit. “Oh.” And we’re through.

The line of cars was also a fun experience. Lots of smiles and waves, given and received.

So Canada. Kind of non-descript place. Lots of corn, very nice rest stops. And it’s weird, the farther we got from the more western states the rest stops got better and better. Wi-fi, restaurants, the like. Pretty much from Iowa on.

We ended up stopping at a giant facsimile of an apple. It was called “the big apple” and it was weird weird weird, but cool in an apple sort of way.

First thing upon entering the site of apple praising and genuflection, you get the high definition television looped 1970’s era promotional video on the creation of said ginormous apple, and it went something like this.

Dude dug pies, dude made building to supply highway goers with awesome pies, dude builds big assed apple on side of highway. Food was alright, but the true highlight was finding out what Poutine is.

First, deep fry French fries (freedom fries, oh Canada fries, chips [in England] etc.). Then sprinkle a liberal amount of mozzarella cheese on it and dump brown gravy on it. SHAZAAM! Poutine. It sounded freaky to me at first, but after only a few straggling fries and blobs of half congealed juice remained, I contemplated my fullness and the distinct possibility that a large chuck of cholesterol was racing towards my heart. But I lived. We ventured into the giant apple, for a majestic view of the kiddy bumper race car things and the already packed up train ride tracks.

So we reached the border of Canada and the United States between 12:30 and 1A.M. on the fifteenth of July. I was freaking out before we arrived. I was trying to come up with a way to hide, conceal, or otherwise carry the little amount of cannabis I had left, really sweating the situation. But it was totally anticlimactic. They were more interested in what fruit and beef we had then anything else. Ten minutes out and away the chuffing commenced again. What a pain in the ass that is, truly. If the united states would only allow themselves to pull their heads out of their collective political asses they would legalize all drugs, tax the shit out of them and be able to subsidize small farmers and large as well across the US to grow whatever they want. Cannabis, opium, have hash bars scattered throughout the US, clean free needles, the whole hemp for life thing. I need to try to get my card, it would allow for a much less stressed me and an equally less stressed wifeykins I'm thinking.

So, smokin', grinning, and watching out for ninja moose, we sped through the Vermontian night. After all the driving it was nice to finally be able to stop driving for a few days.

My time in Vermont has been uniquely singular. After getting more then three to six hours of sleep, a bar-be-que was scheduled for his mothers' birthday.

The whole family converged on the house. Mom, dad, friend from their antique shop, him, his wifey, their two kids, the brother, the brothers daughter, and I. I was interested to meet the family as I had never met them and was interested in the "vermontyness" of it all. They were nice, and fairly congenial, but they began, as the Que progressed, to really haze him on his ability to make money. Constant references to his brother and how much he worked and all, and how since my friend didn't work at a real job (IE internet site) his contribution to the working American force was negligible. At this point I was inclined to speak up. This was pretty much how it went.

"So (brother), how many hours a week do you work?" I ask.

"Ummm. About 50 to 60." He says. (The brother)

"Wow. That sux. "I say." Not much time to spend with your kid huh?"

"Yeah" he says" I guess so."

"Well you know what?" I asked. "See him (friend) cutting that steak?"

"Yeah" Says the brother.

"He just made money." I say.

The father speaks up, as he's the most vocal of the disparagers." Well sure, if a quarter is making money."

"Ah." Says I "he's making a quarter right now as he's cutting his kids steak. He also made a quarter while he cooked the food, while he went shopping, while he ate his food, while he sleeps, while he uses the toilet, while he washes the car, while he goes to his children's plays or school productions, while he reads a book."

After that the conversation seemed to change to other topics, and I got a gratified look from both him and his wife (my friends).

It's hard to blame them for their outlook, especially coming form that area of the states and also the fact that the family is definitely patriarchal. His father seems to come from an era not unlike my own father, yet my father has grown away from that kind of thinking and has become, to his credit, somewhat of a renaissance man.

Adieu

10:29 A.M.

7/20/07

Heading to Burlington from Kirby

Its drop off time for the mother. We're heading to the airport to send her on her flight. He's already starting the whining and weird fallacious arguments.

So entering Vermont. I'm not sure if it was the fatigue, the cannabis, or the night, but that first night in Vermont was full of weirdness. We ended up touching down in front of his casa at approximately 2:30 or 3A.M. Got the tour of his house, nice place, and we both headed back to the RV. After smoking a bowl he suggested we walk up the road outside his house. Now all roads pretty much in that area of Vermont (referred to as the North East kingdom) is criss-crossed by a veritable spider web of dirt roads. They remind me of roads in the desert. Lonely roads, not known if inhabited or not, driving deep into the heart of wild emptiness. It's just that up here in Vermont, its wetter. Ahh, musings on a wet Vermont day.

And so, up the road we go, doobie already burnin', to brave the dark cave of the road through the trees. We came down his driveway which intersected with the road. A little garage type thing across the road with one of those bright sensor lights, that's always on, blazing from it shining onto his driveway. Now his driveway sloped down past his second house over a "brook duct" (one of those pipes that are buried in driveways to be able to cross in a car with no ill effects to stream or car.) and onto the darkened road. We headed right, up the road, and began to cross through and out of the pool of light cast by the security bulb.

Now up here the nights, due to a total lack of any real congestion of population, are actual nights. So when I say we went from the light to the darkness, we went from light into total blackness. I had my three D cell maglite with me and had my finger on the button so to say and he and I delved into the darkness. As we headed up the road we went by the house that owned the garage of spotlightedness, and began to cross a small bridge that allowed for the stream to continue on its way, I saw what I thought looked like something in the road. Now being a hiking, camping kind of guy, the response I have to little critters is to light them up, to be able to fix their location and all and also to let them know, in case my human stench isn't enough, that I'm there. Every other time I've done that a raccoon or possum or some type of critter has appeared, bathed in what I affectionately call my "god" light. This was the time of nonatypicalness. The light from my halogen bulb, three cell D mag "god" light fell on the ground only. Now before the use of the light both he and I had thought something was there. After the light looked to reveal nothing, he began to move forward with a confident "Oh, there's nothing there." And I moved the light away, but still felt certain something was there. I figured it must be something in the glasses that was causing weird reflections, but as I moved the light away I saw the same thing and then it turned and looked at me. I stopped dead in my tracks and asked if he had seen it. He had, for he stopped as well, and as I put the light on it again it didn't show up at all. I began to back off of it and as I did I moved the light off of it again. As I did whatever this thing was it used the light as an actual medium and moved the light from its "tail" down its back to its "head" in a vibrating pattern.

Now in my life I've seen some pretty interesting things. In my life I've experienced things that I have to say defy the "normal" aspects of today's conservative society. But I've never seen anything quite like this before. As it used the light as almost as a liquid medium, like a dog shaking off water. It starts at the head and moves down. This thing moved tail forward while using the light in the same way. It seemed like a monkeyish thing. It sat in the road, when we could see it, with a certain simian quality to it.

So this thing does its shimmy, I stop in my tracks, then it teleports (for want of a better word) over to my feet and around me and then its gone. I take a minute to come to grips with this strangeness as he continues up the road. I figure "Well, it didn't hurt me, was only curious, and since its bizarre but non threatening I'm good and shall continue on." And that all lasted about 5 seconds.

That monkey thing must have been a familiar or a sentry, merely there to call attention to other things that must have been using it or had summoned it for this purpose alone. As we continued up the road I began to feel a weight press down upon me. It was as if the trees were using their age and mass to threaten and drive me from them. Have you ever had that feeling when you go into an old building, or you're somewhere, maybe a party or something, and you get a feeling that you should leave? And maybe you ignore it. And as you ignore it the feeling and the weight continues to mount till you actually physically bend under the pressure? This was the most intensive feeling I had ever felt, and as I tried to continue up the road I felt it more and more and more. It began to bend me double and as I got closer to the ground and more and more hunched and bent I couldn't stand it anymore. I tried to go one more step and the pressure released and there were spirits in the road now. Two that I could "see". One was male, and he was aggressive and irritated that I was there. But further up the road there was a female that I could sense and she was watching inquisitively. The male would jump to me and push his face into mine over and over. As this all progressed I repeatedly told them I was with my friend and I was invited. Over and over I repeated myself, but to no avail. They were pissed for some reason and I was not going to hang out. I spun around on my feet, and ran all the way back to the RV, where I began to cleanse it and myself with sage. The bummer was that his wife didn't dig the smell at all and they spent forever trying to rid themselves of it.

He entered the RV not long after I did and I immediately cleansed him and started to babble at him. My impressions, my thoughts, what I was "picking up" from whatever was out there.

It seemed to be his grandfather of all people and the woman that was supposedly a witch that had owned a still on the mountain up the road. Supposedly his grandfather had been involved with this woman for some time and had a physical relationship with her. I also had impressions of a stagecoach road on the hill up from their house through the woods.

Now as I began to describe the man, the woman, and my impressions of what they wanted his eyes began to grow wider and wider. Now this isn't the first time, nor do I believe it will be the last for me. I found out later he went into his house when we had finished our little chat and had grilled his wife to know if she had told me anything about their family. As she hadn't he tripped out and realized that there may be more then he thought there was in the world.

So that was my first night in Vermont, and what a night it was. Things calmed down somewhat after that and we went up the road in the night and the day after that. We checked out the place where he grew up and where he and his brother would hang out and play.

During my trip to Vermont we went to a few places of note. I'll try to recall and commit those moments to paper now.

Lake Champlain

Went with the whole family to Lake Champlain. Was interesting. Took the boat tour and started drinking right off the bat. Looked for Champ everywhere but didn't see him. As with everything here there is so much history it's impossible to recall everything. I remember lots of naval battles, native peoples (least where they used to be), and cute international women on the ship.

The Flume/Franconia Notch State Park

This place is incredible. It's a large notch taken out of the bare rock with massive amounts of water cascading over the rocks. You're able to walk along a sturdy yet slightly unnerving walkway right along it and above it as well. When I think of Vermont or even the eastern area of the states I think Franconia Notch.

The House of Robert Frost

That's right. Went to the house that bobby chill wrote in for ever and ever. I actually got to touch the chair where he sat and wrote, got to touch the wooden writing tray thing he made to write on in the chair. Seeing the pictures of him sitting in that chair makes me think that he got the short chair and somewhere there's an average height man sitting in a chair that makes him look like he's four years old at the kitchen table.

The house is small and tight in places and seems like it was built for a race of people much smaller then the normal folk of today. And yes, I saw the deep dark woods of his eastern lands and was enlightened.

Burlington

After the Lake Champlain trip we hung out in downtown Burlington. It reminded me of other college towns somewhat in its atmosphere and its street performers. People with carts, white faced balloon sellers, head shops, and all the things that make up small town American tourista.

Other Obscure Things I Noticed or Heard

At a butcher shop in St. Johnsburry

"I'm the carpenter here. Been standin' in this spot right here for twenty two years. Most people don't know meats like wood. Gotta cut ninety degrees to the striations in the muscle."

Christian bookstore turned into a head shop.

Was able to hug a maple tree at the Lyndon Institute, Vermont

Burke View/Lunch

"Please be advised. Drinking of beer and/or alcohol on city street, even in brown paper bags, is illegal and you are subject to a fine and/or arrest."

North Concord

Met a guy that my friend has known for years. Has a tinkering club that tweaks out lawnmowers to race on the ice on a lake that his house is built near. Now they take these riding lawnmowers and they make them go at almost impossible speeds. We're talking fifty five miles an hour. One he said goes up to one hundred miles an hour. They call themselves Drunk Monkey Racing. I beg and am allowed the chance to ride one. The pace is threateningly frightening yet exhilarating.

The DMV in St. Johnsburry

Now to be able to go to the DMV in the small rural township my friend inhabits you must first travel over to the next town, which in this case happens to be St, Johnsburry. Now when you arrive, and it's every Thursday, you need to go to the Elks club and head to the banquet room. Amid the old and not so old pictures of white men in ties and coats, you'll find the laptops humming and the DMV workers working. Actually hung out with the woman that was helping the friend. Sweet lady with multiple kids. Invited her to come out to the RV for a toke or twelve, but she declined. Non rippus at workus. Now if you miss the DMV there, you must drive an hour and a half to Mt. Pellier.

Just past Wilihby Lake

A little of the Vermontian lawn decor. There is the bottom half of a fisherman facsimile falling head first out of a boat by the side of the road. He's falling into the grass that landscaped around it.

The Trip Back

Late in the evening and almost the morning we road again south to White River Junction. I had a bus to catch and couldn't be late. As we got to the bus station there was a guy hanging out at the station, standing quite still and looking out into space. We asked him if the bus had arrived or not and he didn't respond, move, or twitch in any way at all. I began to laugh and realized that it was a three day eleven hour trip on the bus ahead of me and experiences would abound. And they did.

I slept pretty much off and on till we got out of New Jersey and into New York. That bus station is quite huge and the food is nominal. Now unbeknownst to me, the bank account was dry and I had to survive off of granola bars and cheap cheap food on the way back, so I lost some weight.

In Topeka Kansas on a dark night we all heard some grief occurring outside the bus. It went a little something like this.

"What are you doing?" asks the bus driver.

"Hey man, get out from under my bus!" exclaims the bus driver.

Man pulls knife on bus driver.

Bus driver runs like a bunny with the reflexes of a mongoose.

All of us got off the bus and confronted the man who then dropped the knife and turned and ran towards the road. Now for a little background on the geography of the bus station versus the rest of Topeka. The bus station is located not a block away from the police station which happened to be the direction the fellow was traveling. After all the police cars screeched into the parking lot and the cops popped out with guns drawn and the smokers vacated the bus to carcinogate we watched as the fellow, sans knife, was helped (don't bump your head) into the police car.

In Kansas City Missouri an old Spanish woman was getting a hassle because she had taken two seats and the greyhound people were trying to stuff us all into the bus not unlike the induction of sardines into the can. She was trying to speak to the operator and the other personnel but they for some reason took quite some time to get a translator for her. When they finally did they figured out that she had been trying to tell them she had bought two tickets, one for her and one for her son, yet her son didn't come with her. She had two tickets so she thought she was allowed to have two seats. And wouldn't you know it; it took your intrepid informer to begin to write in the little notebook and begin to ask names before they allowed her to sit in her two seats alone. But then, I guess to push the envelope a little farther, she wanted to keep one of the tickets to return it for the money she spent on it. Wily little woman.

I think it was Denver, Colorado where I met a few kids that were heading west. One was a guy from Louisiana. He had been in Louisiana when the hurricane Katrina hit and was not in the least delighted with the response and care that FEMA had given to the citizenry of that state. He talked of many families stuffed into two bedroom trailers and left there. He talked about the fears he had of being stuck in the jail, he was incarcerated, and whether he'd be able to get out. He was released at about the three hour mark for the landfall of the storm. Which according to most sources is consistent with the judicial system.

I met a girl that popped Ritalin like crazy because it allowed her to be calm. From her I got that people in Denver like massage therapists, least the rich ones she said, and that the show supernatural looks insane.

There was a Hispanic guy that traveled all the way to LA with me, and he was going to meet his family I think. Funny guy with a great sense of humor. He had a great liking for the rap music and let me check out the CD's he had.

Met a guy from "Brooklyn New York born and raised!" as he put it. We sang songs to each other that got the younger crowd confused and we chuckled and laughed until he left us in Vegas.

Met a guy, somewhere in the Midwest, that spoke like a younger Sam Elliot. Maybe not the same timbre, but definitely had the cadence down.

So that's the end of it. I arrived in San Luis Obispo, little lighter in the waist yet heavier in the head. I ran off the bus and held tight to my lovely bride, the wifeykins of all wifeykins and the mother of my beautiful children. And yes, I tried the grope, can't help myself. I honestly blame her everyday for being so damned hot. We went to a little hole in the wall hamburger joint called

Sylvester's. Had a great burger and some fries, along with some fried mushrooms as well. And then my life as an at home dad continued.

Now this experiment I did, with the writing and chronicling of my experiences and trip across the U.S. was the first in a long line of gonzoish writings I've been trying to do. It has continued as I've written on my site about concerts, and Fan Faires, and all manner of trips and voyages. But to Vermont, this was the first. The original voyage into the unknown.

Are you glad you came along?

<u>Christopher-</u>
<u>Here's to</u>
<u>"geeking out</u>
<u>on words"</u>
<u>all the best</u>
<u>Suzanne</u>
<u>Cal poly 2008</u>

"Are ya sure you don't wanna go?", I said.

"You'll be missing out on something", the wifey said.

"Naaaaaahhhhhhh…" My darling cherubic daughters response makes me laugh and I say "love ya " to them all and I'm out the door. Already took the trash out, with the wife's help, and I showered for fear of killing by gaseous cloud and I'm ready.

I hop into the "new" car and set up the MP3 player so it'll play some killer tuneage and I smoke a little bowl as I head to Cal Poly. I have at least an hour to go till the poet heads out to poet herself, and I'm wondering if my teacher will be able to make it. I definitely wish my daughter would have wanted to go, but now I can concentrate on the recollection. No distractions of bathroom breaks or hunger. It's once again a solo thing for dad and I'm heading to the college.

I'm glad that my teacher had read the poetry to me and I have a definite preconceived idea of what is going to happen. Or at least what I'm going to encounter. I had the pleasure of witnessing the speaking enchantment of Ray Bradbury at PCPA in Santa Maria once and so I understood the format if not the players. But the real quest was finding exactly where the building was that the speaking engagement was to be in.

California Polytechnic University for some reason seems to be quite confusing and random, like most universities it seems, so I went from here to there and from there back to here and finally found the joint with at least fifteen minutes to spare. I had taken a slight detour after truly finding the place to be able to see if the road to Poly canyon was still open and deduced that the road with the gate on it had been the one. This also adds more time for my loadashunal properties.

I went back to the place and parked the car, put on my newly tye-dyed overcoat and the MP3 player went into the ear. As I went into the building my teacher and her hubby walked up behind me and I hold the door for them. I see her lips moving yet all I hear are Jello Biafra and Ministry jamming as Lard in my ear, Sylvestre Matuschka to be exact, so I poop out the earbuds and she's introducing me to her hubbykins. Nice guy. Quiet. Which is funny because that would be anyone's response to anybody they exchange two words with. We wander around the joint until a guy takes pity on us and leads his newly found flock to the correct door. There are the two ladies in the back selling stuff that the authors are trying to pimp on us and the newly arrived, us. The others, teacher and her hubs and some other older gentlefolk congregate down near the front, bout row two or three. I head back to the spot that I claim anywhere and everywhere. The back left.

Now this is a funny arrangement I have with myself. I seem to do this now almost subconsciously, but I know I'm doing it, and I do it for a number of reasons. One is that I can see the entire room, at all times. Partly a "back never to the door" thing and a way to be able to see the interaction of everybody in the room. How they respond to something. How they look at each other. Where they go themselves to sit. All these things enter into it. So I sit, they sit, and the waiting begins.

As people filter into the room we see hugging between the older crowd, semi-mingling and other attachments. I'm looking for someone from class, anyone at all really, just to see if anyone shows up but me. Other filter in, the wait continues, younger crowd now coming in. I see a little princess outside the door to the outside, not the other that leads to the inner sections of the building. She dodges out into sight, looks in the room a bit, and walks to the other side of the doorway. She's barefoot and has a tiara of ribbon on.

After the second hot redhead comes in I switch the tunes to Blue Oyster Cult and song "Black Blade". I think the woman with the dyed hair is the poetess I'm here to see and I confirm this when my teacher gets up and hugs her. The poetess seems genuine as does my teacher in their happiness to see each other and their friendship is apparent. The poetess and an older dude go up to the podium and he speaks into the mike lauding praise on his "past student". She welcomes it all fairly graciously and takes his place after getting someone to move the mike stand back a bit. She says she knows she's loud enough without the mike and her following laughs. Then she begins to speak.

Most of the poems she read were ones that my teacher had read previously to the class and they were different just slightly. My teacher, to her praise I might add, did do them justice and made me interested to see the woman actually do her art herself.

I pick up on her lisp first, yet that falls away as she gets into it. Maybe its subconscious, one of those "feigned disabilities" that are spoke of of women in the past. Perhaps. Maybe I'm just waxing poetic for no other reason then I've been inundated tonight. Speech pattern aside she really rises into her words and her love for her "brain children" and her education and her mother is beautiful to watch. The room is taken over by her, all of her and I wonder now remembering back if she even knows that at that moment she was in the "be". Her own "be" that she wrote about. With the weird quirk biases aside I find her moments tonight magnificent.

The man after her was fine, not unlike hair, but not at all the commanding spirit that she had. His story was interesting, which is what we're told to say to be nice to people, but he kind of drones a bit and the specifics in his story are unneeded. He adds and adds when his audience knows the direction he's going already. We knew the watch was there, we needed to get there sooner. But it was enjoyable.

Afterwards there is a question and answer period where they try to answer the unanswerable questions to where it comes from and I sit there and answer the questions as well in my head. My answers are different then theirs. They speak of editing for years and changing their poetry and their stories and I'm totally confused. How can they edit? I hate editing and find it troublesome and irritating and totally irresponsible to their brain children. I can't do it, but sometimes I do, so I guess it's all a lie. Hmmmmm…

I go up and buy her book and get her to sign it. I steal a pen for a second from the old ladies pimping the stuff and walk up to her. I ask her to sign it and she agrees but she's got her own pen already. I take the pen I "stole" back to the ladies and hang out by a pillar because she's delayed for a second coming up to the table to talk to the sellers. She gets there, does her biz, and turns to me to sign it.

"Are you a writer?" she asks.

"From time to time I am a word geek, yes I am." I respond. Why I'll never know.

"Well, okay." And she signs it.

My teacher came up at the time that she's signing it and introduces me to her friend the poetess, and says I'm the only one in her class. I agree that I'm the "token" male and the poetess tells of a military gentleman in her class that said it was all about man bashing and lesbianism. My mind says "bizarre" and my mouth smiles. For some reason her eyes are not on either her friend, my teacher, or me at all. They seem to be roaming left and right from my teacher to the others to her left and back again. I say thank you to the poetess and move my way out of the building. As I pas my teacher I ask her exactly what she wants and she gives me free range, with a parting "it can be stream of consciousness if ya want", with a smile on her space. This refers to a final paper I talked to her about and I laugh and say that I'm still not sure if I'm going to follow through with that idea yet.

I get in the car and start it up and the MP3 player with Aero by Jean Michelle Jarre and I take off. I park for a sec at the permit station on highland and call the fam to see if they want anything. There's no pick up on the other end and I can only trail off for so long. I hang up and have a toke or two and drive back home.

SOE Fan Faire

Or, How I Got To Hang Out With My Bruthah From Anothah Muthah at the Geek Fest of Geek Fests

So there I was. Anticipating a great time yet nervous about it at the same moment. My brother and I were heading to the SOE fan faire in Las Vegas, and his ultimatums (no drugs {cannabis} and no strippers {it's been at least 18 years since my libido, in connection with my body, entered a strip club}) were kind of a hassle since I entered into no dire ultimatums with him. Yet I had agreed to the terms and was packed and ready to go. After calling my mom and letting her know about the website and how to get there, a needed thing as anyone with computer illiterate parents knows, I grabbed the back pack and the flight bag and went outside. The plan was my sister was to arrive any moment, she was at least a half hour late, and I was to get a ride with her down to the broskie-in-law's place of employment, then from there we would motor down to his mothers house where his children would be cared for by her, therefore giving his wifey, my sis, a break for a few days. So I went out the door of the apartment I share with my beautiful wife and children, locking it behind me, and headed out to meet the sister so she wouldn't have to come to the front door to get me.

I sat by the back end of the car and whipped out the notebook I've been carrying for about a month so far and as Murphy's Law states she shows up. I load it all back in to the pack, and climbed in the van. The niece and nephew were spazzin pretty much as always, the sister and I vary on our views on children and caffeine, and so I tried to let it all wash over me as we sped down the road to the bro-in-law.

We got to his job, loaded up the car with kids uncle's bro-in-law's and packs, suitcases, and we went on our way. The ride was not too painful to the bro-in-laws mothers' casa, though there was in my mind a slightly perverse amount of the Christian tune thing goin on. Since I hadn't done the "ultimatum" thing and hadn't brought any of the serious thrash metal "devil" music as my unenlightened family puts it, I begged repeatedly for other music(I would have accepted jazz at this point), but then we arrived and hugs were handed out and lunch was grinded down, whence his father arrived. Lunch imbibed, hugs once again were handed out and we, as they say, got on down got on down, down the road.

The ride from the central coast area of California is sort of pleasant and painful all at once. As a traveler you're leaving the great Pacific Ocean for the desert, yet in the desert is Vegas, the ultimate in freaky adult entertainment. The true saving grace was that we entered the desert in the evening, so it was relatively cooler (98billion degrees versus 110billion degrees) and the desert in the night is a truly beautiful yet strange and disturbing place. It seems as if as you cross the mountains and you climb through them you find Joshua trees and other types of cacti and it seems as if you've entered an alien landscape. Another world stretches before you, the landscape sere and scorched yet beautiful and stark. In the winter it snows here in the high desert, the weird gates across the freeway attest to that, and yet in the summer the temperature climbs into the triple digits. We talked of different things like religion and the amount of drinking I was thinking I would do, listened to a little coast to coast AM I had on CD along with some other music (the Christian stuff had been shelved) that I had brought with me. Most of it was synthesizer stuff Jean Michel Jarre, some Orb I had gotten my hands onto; nice smooth catchy stuff, and the desert flowed by. Some traffic slowed us a bit out there before Baker which then smoothed back out again and we rolled into Vegas around 2:30 in the AM.

The next morning at 8:30 in the AM we got some cereal and some juice at the little store in the time share my sis and bro had acquired a few years ago which was where we were staying, and had breakfast. Knock-off frosted wheat squares and I had a rum and juice mixed drink. Now I'm not necessarily a heavy drinker, I'm much more of the hemp kinda guy, but after reading a forum on the fan faire and the posts indicating the amount of booze that seemed to flow through these things I was taken it to the limit. In retrospect, I was a light weight compared to some and a little more intense in comparison to others. So with a slight gurgle in my gullet, a pack a cigars in the pocket
(which since I was on a slight hiatus from my imbibitions of choice there was no other smokable) we drove over to the Rio where the faire was held. And to be honest I take my hat off to the people of Las Vegas that can stand the heat that they have to live in out there in that weird desert adult play land. But I don't take it off for long, my head would burn.

So now for those of you out there that have never been to Las Vegas, it's a bizarre place. The heat would kill if it wasn't for the gigantic turbine like coolant towers that feed these casinos allow for an artic cool within the opaque glass of their doors. So being a total complete and utter Californian (I packed nothing but tie-dyes, yes that was me) it took a few minutes to acclimate from the outside temperatures to the inside temperatures. And then the stench of barely hidden and cleansed from the air of stale smoke, even with a cigar in hand, is almost too much to bear. But we made it to where the line began for the check in and since we had already both paid way early, it was an uneventful wait. The guy behind us had been at the start, of all things, of the cannonball run. Now being sports retarded, self imposed of course, I was amazed that the run was an actual race let alone one allowed in the US. He told us that it had been many years since the race had been held in the US and it had just got back from Europe where the laws on speed in a car, and most all else, was less stringent. We saw pictures and some cell phone mini videos of some of the cars taking off, rolling over the asphalt "donuts" left there by the arrivals the night before. One of the SOE event staff (as the faire progressed I would find there was many of them) came over and asked what our character names were, took them down, and others were busily behind the counter getting the badges ready for the faire participants. Everyone in line was courteous and not at all pushy or obnoxious so it was a gentle wait. The people in front of us were talking, quite animatedly I might add, about SWG and the ways for space combat and what the PVP and PVE states were and how they worked them to their advantage.

Was interesting for me being a primarily fantasy RPGer and being there for EQ2, but not enough to actually play it.

So after the SWG fest-o-info we moved along in the line, not unlike cattle to a slaughter house, and got our badges. Yes. We needed stinking badges. Then off to the swag (I still feel it should be pronounced shwag, yet my bruthah said nonononono..swag is swag. And to truly give him credit, he let me know what the hell swag means…Stuff We All Get. At least that was his angle and it seemed a good one) counter for a shirt and some stuff. As we were waiting at the swag counter, one guy was trying to get us to grab the paper bags with the Station logo on it while the other guy was trying to figure out whether we had all the swag(shwag) or not. Needless to say, I waited till the crisis was abated. So with all our stuff in tow, in bag, and swagged up, we unleashed ourselves into the official 2007 SOE fan faire.

And then we went drinking. There was a big room, "booths" were set up along the sides, yet it was reminiscent of an almost senior prom thing, kinda. All the people milling around the center of the room, getting into lines for raffle ticket turn ins, doing surveys, pictures for a SOE thing if you have an interesting story thing to post or something. Took about a half an hour to cruise around and then we were done. At least for the moment, and it was time for drinking. They had multiple bars set up around the fan faire, probably to enhance the buying power of their players that were attending, and the prices were astonishing. For a small tumbler of rum and coke, and it was clear Bacardi only at most of the places, was $8.50. Now being a struggling student and not a high dollar kinda guy with two kids I couldn't afford the prices for consecutive drinking incursions, so what to do? Well, here's the trick, when yer in Vegas and yer low on cashola, sit yerself down at the penny slots in whatever casino you happen to be in. Place a 5 dollar bill into the receptacle, bet every line you can on the screen, at the lowest bet per line possible, and begin to look thirsty. And really, ya wanna look REAL thirsty. As soon as the drink guy or girl comes by, ya ask for 2 of whatever ya want, because who knows how long it will be till they return to fill your thirsty order again. That's the key for pretty much any casino, but at the RIO I definitely take my hat off to them. They know not only how to do a decent fan faire pool party (I promise I'll get to that) they make sure that no matter how much money yer losing, I mean playing, they make damn sure you have a drink while your doing it. So after many rum and cokes, and I think my bruthah was goin the rum and cokes as well, but later on the next day he switched over to Newcastle brown ales for stomach reasons, and we returned to the fan faire for a live event.

The entire fan faire had a slightly hectic feeling to me of almost but not quite falling completely into disarray and dissolution. There were almost a 4 to one ratio in "event staff" to attendees, though I suspect that the event staffers where not all SOE employees. Yet when asked questions you sometimes had to go to two or three people before you got a sufficient answer.

So, there we are, feeling pretty good, and we have to go around the area where the fan faire was and try to find people with feathers above their heads. That's right all you EQers and EQ2ers, we were looking for NPC's to hail. Now, when yer feeling slightly toasty and you say hail to like 8 people about 20 times each, one becomes much more inventive. "Hard precipitation!" was one of my favorites, and as my bruthah was is and always shall be Sleet, his was a name that was called not only for recognition, but also for NPC attention.

So the live event for EQ2 was fun, had to solve word search puzzles, had to talk to an ogre (who had a severe hatred of bandana's) a slightly effeminate high elf, and a militant erudite (who was actually a long hair in this tortuous world of reality), among others. After the quest detritus was collected we headed back into the room where we originally got our group of ten and the instructions for the quest. I think we were trying to get into Nerriak. The group we (my bruthah and I) had was a good group a folks. A couple guys, one younger then the other but both fairly boisterous, and a girl and two other guys that knew each other, along with two other guys one tall one middling height. The two we met from blackburrow and the three from oasis were the ones that we (my bruthah and I) eventually hung out with for the rest of the fan faire, when we weren't checkin the pulse of Vegas outside of the realm of SOE and the fan faire. So after the live event we decided, what the hell, lets go check out the star trek experience at the Hilton. Now for a couple of super freak geeks like us, there was no place so like a pilgrimage through the heat and toil of the Vegas afternoon and the congestion of traffic to be able to walk into the cool and technical beauty of that place. It was our Mecca, our Shangri-La, our pleasure dome.

When you first walk into the place you realize that you have to stop walking forward to acclimate correctly to the sub artic temperature that most casinos in Vegas have. They actually build strange turbines and buildings to be able to combat the heat of the Vegas desert. Then you look up, and to the side, and you realize that you have walked into a strange world. There are people walking around you, beautiful women, chiseled men, and then there's that Borg over there. No. over there by the Ferrengi. That's the strangeness.

We walked up to the counter to get our tickets and of course, it being Vegas, we're asked if we need help. We both run the "how much for what "thing and the guy gives us the greatest help I've ever had in a casino or anywhere else except for Disneyland. I'll try to remember it for ya here…

Us.."What kind of discounts do you have? AAA?"

Him.."Sure. AAA is good, but there are better ones."

Us.."Ok..And where does one get these said discounts of greater discountyness?"

The live event helped to get us prepared I tell ya.

Him…"Well. I'm not supposed to tell you that if you walk out to the monorail, and look for a kiosk, and look in one of the magazines out there, I'm not supposed to tell you that you'll find greater discounts in there."

Us…"Well thank you for not telling us these things and therefore jeopardizing your job." As we tried not to giggle like freaky late 30's early 40's school children and followed his explicit non directions to said non kiosk and found said non discounts. After acquisition of said non discounts we went up to the counter and realized we had got ourselves 16 dollars off of the main price tag. So with tickets in our pockets and lightness in our steps we headed into the experience.

Now from the roof are suspended a gigantic model of the Enterprise, the Voyager, and a Klingon bird of prey. There is a walkway that winds up into the area that the “ride” takes place at that has the entire time line from the beginning of the star trek universe to the end of it. For the record that’s from Copernicus to I think the data jump across the two ships in Nemesis. So now, as we walk up further into the bowels of the experience, the perma grins on our faces are starting to hurt. We’re seeing the suits, on quite provocative plastic mannequins, of the two Klingon sisters from Generations. We’re seeing the actual suit that the shape shifter dude wore in deep space nine. It’s a complete and utter geek festival for me and my bruthah. So we’re standing in the enterprise experience line and the guy in front of us starts in on the “If you have a Borg experience ticket, come forward. There’s only a few seats available and we’re leaving soon.” Which he repeats about 8 times and yet we deviate not a jot from our intended task and we remain in line for the star trek experience.

Now at this point will I actually tell you what happens? No, of course I won’t. Let’s just say the smile of total and complete geek satisfaction on each of our faces is huge and uncompromising. As we head out the exit to the ride we enter, after the star trek shops where single episodes on DVD are 20 bucks a pop, we went to Quarks bar. Now for those of you that are not in the “know” Quark was a Ferrengi character on Deep Space Nine that was, as his race decrees, a shiftless horse trader of the lowest degree. And I mean that as a compliment. Within this bar of bars we, my bruthah and I, were savy enough to split the 30 dollar cost of a "Warp Core Breach". Now this drink comes with 5 different kinds of rum and is served in a 10 gallon goldfish bowl with its own little holder for said bowl. It was worth EVERY PENNY. The taste was exquisite and the fact that they serve it with dry ice so it bubbles like a witch's brew from hell was just the sort of perk that we wanted, needed, and deserved. After we shot the incriminating photo and got to downin this thing the buzz was pleasant and not too overwhelming. Kinda one a those were ya know ya feel buzzed, but it takes about 7 steps to truly know the extent of the buzz and that it'll take at least three hours and some water from the ever present Nalgene bottle at my side to be at least remotely able to drive again. So why not do the Borg?

We did the Borg and we did them well. And yes, it's another ride I refuse to tell you all about. It was awesome and a requirement to any trekker to ensure that at some point they get to Vegas and do the gambit. And don't forget to hit the Bar and have a drink.

So we realized that as our buzz subsided somewhat it was time to head back to the time share we were at, thanks to my bruthah, and get into our swim suits and head back down to the Rio and hit the pool party. Being the frugal bastard that I am I was not going to get financially screwed for a buzz, especially since I had bought approximately 50 bucks worth of good rum for this trip. So I made a wickedly powerful concoction, also incased in Nalgene, and we went for party time.

Now out of the entire weekend, sans the side trips and all with the bruthah, the Rio knows how to throw a great pool party. Now short of parties by a friend's pool growing up, I had not had a chance to attend a pool party especially in Vegas, so I was quite excited. And it was nothing like what I was expecting. I kept looking at the crowd thinking, "wow. Lotta drunk geeks here huh? Better get started on my buzz and better get my bruthah to come along as well". So I, we, us did get started on a good buzz that lasted quite through the night. There was karaoke going as we entered the party area and someone was doing a rendition of "pour some sugar on me" from def leopard. But it wasn't any suck assed karaoke; they had an actual band playing instruments behind you as you sang. The only drawback was that they didn't play for long enough in my mind, but they were excellent musicians and quite a part of the whole pool party experience. The song I remember from the party were Ramones-I wanna be sedated/Iron Maidens-The Trooper/ NIN-Head like a hole/ GnR-Sweet child of mine and Mr. Brownstone. All with the band sweating and jamming behind the geek of the moment, spinning and freaking out on stage to the rapture and joy of the rest of us. But the real fun happened when, half an hour after we finished the drink and my bruthah was feelin like crap (too quick with the booze was the dual consensus later) and we were sitting by the side of the pool the rest of our live event group showed up and one of em, the guy I affectionately dubbed "Mr. Intense" offered to buy me a drink. Not being a guy to turn down a libation in pretty much any form, I acquiesced and he returned with a gut wrenching painful looking shot of Jack Daniels. I unshackled my Nalgene of water and began to prepare for the burn when he said, "Wow..free bar man". To which I replied (after quaffing the shot in one gulpo) "Well I better get started then!" And I did. I began, as at the penny slots, to two fist the drinks down as much as possible, as my bruthah caught a good buzz off of the Newcastle vibe (I believe this is where it started and remained for the rest of the trip) and we hobnobbed with our new found comrades. You all that were there, let me know if you want me to include your names (EQ names only of course) in this blog and I will where applicable. There were two women dressed up as EQ/EQ2 toons that had begun to party before we even arrived and were actually walking behind me and my bruthah while we were on our way to the pool party. They were a saucy pair of flirts that truly brought an excellent and vibrant feel to the party. The sad thing is that we didn't see them again after that night and I hope they were not reprimanded for anything they did or said.

So there we were, drinkin by the pool, and as the booze began to flow, the geeks began to submerge, to which I used the affectionate term "geek soup" which the pool began to become. And then the "lets throw (blank) in!" began and my bruthah was quick to doff his shorts down to the suit for swimming and submerge his bulk. What a trend setter I tell ya, because as I followed suit and got in the pool it was deliciously cool and satisfying against the skin. Even at night the heat in Vegas is blistering. The heat is actually blistering at all moments and never seems to lighten up at least as far as the times I've been there.

The karaoke ended and the geek herding began. The old adage "you don't have to go home but you can't stay here" was in full force and the security was literally doing the hands outstretched duck/goose/chicken herding arms outstretched angle and the geeks were blearily working their way out the doors and into the Vegas midnight. I was invited to come up to the room of our live event friends so my awesome bruthah took us back to the time share where we doffed our wet shorts and donned our dry ones. Then he drove me back to the Rio where one of the live guys was staying and I went in.

Now after that many rum and cokes it was difficult to remember the room number. It was either 1831 or 1381 and so I decided, after asking the desk staff to call the room and realizing after I asked that it was after 1 am in the morning, to start at the top and work my way down. Now if I ever meet the poor people that were staying in room 1831 I would, after apologizing profusely, declare that in my inebriated state it was an honest drunken mistake. And yet, if it had been me, I would find it hard to forgive a nights lack of sleep in the midnight lights of Vegas. So, after bangin on the door for a short 15 to 20 minutes and realizing that I didn't have my bruthahs cell phone number, nor the number of any in the group, I was hosed and would be walking with a chilled bottle of Captain Morgan's private stock rum. Good rum and all, but that was a poor salve for the blisters that would form on the feet of your fearless narrator. But then the light that usually forms over the heads of the none too bright in cinema formed over my bleary head and I thought, was it 1831or was it 1381? Since this seemed like a decent quandary to investigate I went down 5 floors and wandered the building.

The door to 1381 was shut but there was the blessed sounds of partying behind it so I knocked on the door and was invited into the room. The pungent odor of cannabis and the blaring sounds of 300 welcomed me into the cacophony. So there was 300 going and then every person other then the only girl there was talking at high volume about , of course, EQ2. The ins, the outs, the everythings. For the next 2 hours there was nothing else discussed. Though being at the fan faire, and meeting everyone in the room at the fan faire, it was not hard to believe that when you throw all us geeks together you get geek talk. So I had a few hits, though the guilt for it was not worth it when later I laid on the fold out sofa blazed and awake in the dark in Vegas, and talked with the others about this and that. The benefits for the scout class and their need for a brutal overkill in agility. (A common thing for me to tell the truth as I am a total agility freak.)

So as the crowd began to fade I caught a ride with a pair of my new found friends back to the time share, but being as how I didn't drive into Vegas, I couldn't find the damnable place I was staying at. So we drove around Vegas while I tried to find the damnable place when, after I gave directions dependent on the amount of construction cranes in the area I was around, I looked back down the street at a red light and saw the small driveway area leading to the room. I had them park at the road and with assurances of tomorrows meeting at the fan faire I staggered slightly down the drive and up to the room and sought unconsciousness.

The next day we woke, somewhat groggily, and made our way down to the fan faire. We wandered around a bit, checking out the stuff they were selling and all, talked to a few of the reps from the online games like burning seas and had lunch with the live event crew. The day being Saturday we, my bruthah and I, spent most of the day playing penny slots and rum and cokes (though bruthah man had switched to Newcastle by now and was doing quite nicely) and jumping between the fan faire and the Rio's shows. The real festivities started at the "banquet" later on. Now when I think of a banquet I think of food, good food, prepared by guys and gals in semi funny hats kinda perched on their heads with the main funny hat guy, probably foreign and holding onto the accent for all he/she's worth, putting little strange designs in chocolate and saying things like "Now she is DONE!". But not SoE. Our banquet, our great feast from a mega company like them was hotdogs and hamburgers. Now I will admit the hotdogs were John Holmes specials in length and the hamburgers were quite tall, I was there for a banquet not a bar-be-que. Yet the greatest part of that whole night was the wedding of two people at the actual fan faire dressed in period renaissance faire kinda garb. They did their vows in front of everyone and then got married in game with their toons. Now the cat calls and jibes at anything and everything that were flying around the pace before this was, at least in my mind, deserved and somewhat expected. The entire fan faire had a tongue and cheek kinda way of running and so after drinking, the costume contest, and their version of a "banquet" I was surprised at the wedding. The hushed reverence while they got married in RL (real life) there was not a jibe or cat call from anyone. There was actually complete and utter silence. Now utter silence in a room filled with a few thousand people is an awesome thing, and when it's for such a beautiful thing as well it means so much more. Personally I and my beautiful wife were married in a justice of the peace 15 minute special, our time with family and friends was a few months later when we had the reception. But each time, the actual wedding and the actual party, there was a love that was felt, I'd think by all, for us and for the aspects of true marriage vows and bonds. That same feeling was there at the fan faire. When they were pronounced man and wife in RL the cheers were deafening and then when their toons got hitched it actually got louder. I shook hands with the proud couple and told them how happy I was to be able to be there and they were graciously kind, not only to me but to everybody.

So after we went out for a quick carcinogen break we went back into the building to check out the dancing and fun. After the pool parties' insanity and fun we all figured there would be some intense fun to be had for the rest of the night. We were wrong. Walking back to the banquet hall it felt like we were the confused salmon on the annual spawning run. We were definitely going against the flood of people exiting the hall. We arrived to Roy Orbison and about 50 drunks shuffling and clinging on the "dance floor" was all that there was left to this gig. It was dead yet no one had had the common decency to tell them about it. So we left and headed out into the Rio and where our feet would take us.

Now there was a strange love triangle thing happening between a few of the live event crew and that seemed to come to a head this evening. At the craps table some intermediate fondling turned into a stomp off and the rest of the night, intermixed with serious amounts of alcohol, was centered around the he and her side and then the he left out side of the triangle, and the he left out side was mostly trying to keep Mr. intense from damaging anyone and/or spending the night in a nice quiet Vegas holding tank. So I drank, and pronounced, and fed the he section some semi cliché yet heartfelt vibes to try to make him feel better, and drank some more.

So by three in the AM it was time to boogey to get at least a modicum of sleep before the long drive back to get the bruthas kids and the life we left behind. So he and I once again cruised back to the room, passed out, and rose again the next day. We went out to get the car from the valet guys, got in, and cruised out to the west, running from the eastern sun and back to the lives we had left for the short time at the SOE fan faire where we could let go and totally geek out.

Essays

A NATION OF MAN

As a child growing up in suburban Arroyo Grande I never hated another person. Well, that's not entirely true. I had my share of dislikes. That guy that punched me, the girl that laughed at me when I threw up in sixth grade class. It was less of a hating or maliciousness and more of a crash course in the aspect of a social pecking order. In fact, when being told a racial or slanderous joke, I wouldn't even get it. After being on the planet for an indeterminate amount of time I came to realize that the human race as a whole would benefit from a non racially biased community.

Now does that mean that white must go, or is it more believable to see the influx of other genetic races and beliefs as a more profitable way to go about it. As a white heterosexual male from a middle class family, the parents taught us, the children, to love one another and to love our common man. Not to readily go out and persecute the "other races" purely because of the color of their skin. It is vitally important to look at the problem of racism as a disease that should be on the world vaccination lists as a number one priority. Can you imagine what would happen if people in general couldn't blame "the white man" for all the countries ills?

Imagine if you will that there is no longer a white majority. Immediately following the downfall of the Caucasian man there ensues a power struggle to fill the void. The liberated Asian front moves to block the power of the African

American Coalition. What makes you think that because the whites are no longer in control and able to tell people what to do, that someone else won't seize the reigns of power and pick up the slack? People of another skin color or ethnicity are in control of the majority vote. It's amazing that people think that once the whites are no longer in power that all the hatred would simply disappear. They are wrong. The power struggle would spread throughout our cities, our towns, even within the fragile borders of the family unit. There would still be pockets of white controlled areas, towns and counties, that would breed even more of the racial hatred and uneducated slanders that make enlightened whites that love their fellow man hang their head in shame. The real power is proper education and love for our fellow man, not who's in charge of what. The hate and fear of histories bloody nostalgia will always influence our actions and our beliefs.

The true mark of the evolution of the race of man as a species would be to throw off the fear we still carry from our genetic ancestors and educate and enlighten ourselves. Experience the joy of the birth of man as a peaceful creature and not as the animal he is, barely above the food chain he preys on hoping the fire won't go out. If you look closely you can see that that is what we as a race are still doing. A few million years go by and we're so busy patting ourselves on the back for building a bigger computer that no one can really use efficiently that we don't realize that we've corrupted ourselves, our children, and our world. We let our lives go bye thinking we're going somewhere or being someone that we lose sight of our right for happiness and in turn we lose the ability to break free of the circle of material gain.

As a free people we founded this country on the melting pot theory, yet where did it go? Have we, in our conquest for genocide like behavior, actually gone forward with that thought beyond the paper it's printed on? If the educational institutions can influx their curriculum with more factual histories instead of the histories written by the conquers, the truth would become a benefit and a resource for the education of a more thoughtful nation. Can you imagine going into a class room for a history lesson on pre-white America taught by a Native American? The students, through the teacher and his knowledge, might come to understand the history of a people that believed in the power of the self and the world around them. Can you imagine a bible literature class taught by a Buddhist monk? Talk about a different interpretation. What would he say of Jesus Christ? Possibly that he was a good story teller.

The important thing to think about and to remember is that we as a race of man need to be able to move past our petty squabbling and look towards the future for our children and their children. We need to break free of the barriers of racial and even religious animosity and move towards the love that we as a people can feel towards one another if we only allow ourselves the chance. As a race of man and woman and in one voice we need to stand up against the hate mongers and love killers and say to them, and to each other, that we want to believe in our common man and trust him with our love. We need to break down the walls of cold war animosity and look to each other for help in recapturing this beautiful planet, and in recapturing ourselves. We need more institutions of enlightenment and education, not hate and fear.

Why is it that when we send an individual to jail, an institution of hate and fear, and then he/she comes out after serving their sentence and are better criminals? Look at what we do to them. We as a society send them to a walled and segregated arena of hate and fear. A place where there are hunters and prey, a place where we can put them behind bars, out of eyesight and earshot, and forget they exist. Years go by, and when we feel that they have served their time for their crime we thrust them back into a world that doesn't want them and a society that has no use for them. We need to break the cycle of shame, abuse, and terror. We as a race must become enlightened and educated so we can instill the correct ethics and moral standing within each individual on Earth.

The main point is that love and understanding can only come from true education from the people involved in the persecution and oppression in our society. Would Rodney King have been beaten so brutally if the cops in question had been all black men? As posed in the question for this essay, it's a matter of demographics. We, the white's , came to this country and persecuted everyone of other color and ethnic distinctions because of fear. When we had that under control we imported people to become prejudice against. Yet are white people somehow exempt from prejudice? No. The man that was beaten so brutally with a brick when dragged from his truck by the black youths in the LA riots was a kind person. After the trials he was seen embracing the mother of the boy that had beaten him. He and the mother were enlightened by love and not historical stories of hate and fear. Love is what needs to be addressed, not the majority in power at this or any future time. We need love for ourselves, for each other, and love for our planet. When we can achieve that end we have moved beyond the need for racial discussions, and are vaulted into the realms of the unknown.

Yet that distant horizon is not unknown to me. It is a horizon that stretches toward a future of understanding between colors. It is a horizon that seems to beckon even now to me with a song, an echo of future possibilities. Listen carefully. You can hear it if you want to, if your able. It's the echo of that song, a minuscule and barely audible portion that sings of love and understanding.

In the immortal words of John Lennon "All we need is love". You know what? John was right all along. All we need is love, that and nothing else.

THE ANCIENT GUARDIAN

The gulls take flight from their homes throwing themselves bodily into space. They wheel and turn as whimsical as leaves in an autumn wind but with a more intent protocol. They want a squirming bloody morsel from the sometimes seasonal, sometimes habitual fisher folk that frequent these waters on the quieter side of the granite god.

I can't see them yet but I know the black skinned fictional seals, and the factual ones, are frolicking in the blue depths of the pacific, artfully dodging rock and danger for a piece of the action. The former, waves. The latter, fish. The gulls pepper the water.

An old man appears in a white Ford truck. He skillfully places each foot into brown rubbers, his hands performing an almost unconscious task. He prepares for his excursion to the watery brine slowly and with patience. He knows that he will not be descending into those cold depths in the flesh, yet the spirit has been known to plunge deeper then the body ever could.

As I look to my left at the huge ancient guardian of the harbor the sun comes like a freight train over the cab of my truck, a ravenous beast that wants to tear at my retina and blind me forever. I angle my head upwards toward the guardian and the beasts anger is lessened somewhat by my sunglasses. The beast creeps back a few steps, yet it will wait for me until its sister drives it from the sky, and then only for a time. Small grey tree-like scrub brush stand like centuries only allowing the worthy to proceed to pay tribute and tithe the ancient granite god. I don't test their resolve and drive to the side facing the harbor.

A small beach, an undisturbed islet ruled by gulls, sprawls before me. A virginal stretch of sand that by night will be consumed by her beau. I can see him now slowly absorbing her into himself swallowing her as the earth, moon, and sun direct his tidal adulations. A fisherman walks slowly across the beach casting his line into the surf his steps breaking her hymen of serenity. The beau of brine cares not for he will have her all for himself very soon now.

I leave my truck, braving the sun beast, and move across the heated tarmac which soon turns to rock. I gaze out at beach and water yet my eyes are drawn to the leviathan of rock. Neither weather, nor time, nor man's pathetic excuse for destruction can dwindle the magnificence of silent power this giant exudes.

I sit alone on a rock on the jetty as salt enriched air runs its playful fingers across my scalp tossing the shadow of my hair across these pages. A lone note peals across the water as if in eulogy for the time long gone, the beaches consumed, and the men swallowed whole and digested by the sands fearsome beau.

He is a jealous one, that beau. I can see and feel the white foaming stallions he sends against the rock of the jetty that now holds me. I sit almost thirty feet from their pounding hooves yet I am in awe of their power. They are ignorant yet insistent beasts slamming against the rocks, plunging through moss and stone again and again and again. They retreat as if to try to fool me, to lull me as a babe in well known arms. I know their game and they will not catch me today.

I move my thoughts and my gaze from their lamentations and anger to the ancient granite mogul that hunches and yet sprawls on my right. The scientists like all "educated" men pushed, probed, pricked, and prodded and explained this hulking majesty away. "A granite plug of a once great volcano now extinct." On their way they went to do experiments on fetal brain transplants in Alzheimer's patients never seeing, never feeling, never truly experiencing this giant.

Two hikers move across the jetty on my right towards the guardian becoming progressively smaller. The guardian never moves, doesn't utter a sound, yet it dwarfs them almost seeming to engulf their frail and insignificant individuality. They perch on a rock close to it and the man makes feeble attempts to grab the girls' thigh, she in turn making equally feeble attempts to fend him off. His hand comes to rest somewhere on her knee.

How often has its edifice looked down on such activities? Does it notice us at all or are we merely specks in its existence moving blindly down through its realm till all its really aware of is the watery beau pursuing his silicone mate through time? I don't know the answer. I merely sit like it does and watch quietly from the wings waiting for the true outcome in all things. Time.

I walk back to my truck. Boulders become rocks, rocks give way to sand, sand in turn changes once again to asphalt.

The fisherman has moved slowly along her small and innocent shore unaware that his footsteps, now so deeply imbedded, will be gone by morning. A couple on my left feed the gulls as they face towards the harbor. The gulls screech insults and indignations at each other as they scramble for their tiny morsels. An old woman to my right gazes through binoculars at the monolith behind me. Does she see the hulking granite god? Is she in awe as she stands before him? No. Her view is captured by birds fighting for space and sustenance on the sprawling ancient guardian. But what pray tell does it see, if anything?

As I back my truck out of my parking space, I roll a smoke and head for home.

Karl and Socrates

The Odd Couple

We begin our story in a dingy one room studio apartment. Socrates has been up all night thinking and chugging Absinthe. Karl, of course, has been trying to get a flight attendant to have sex with him, but she's been hiding in the closet in fear for her sense of privacy. Since Karl's closet was rigged with cameras poised at every angle he's been engaging in a constant masturbatory mania. After he pushes himself out of the collection of used tissues Socrates sees him and their talk begins.

Soc: So what was it you wanted to talk to me about?

Karl: The benefits of lying to the people that we, as you called us, legislators, need to do in order to protect and cherish the order of things.

Soc: But what order can one derive from a society based on lies and deception?

Karl: When Hitler took over in Germany, after the fall of the Huns and the dissolution of her people in the beginning of this century, if he had said to the people of that fine country that the way to a more perfect unification was to burn people in large ovens, the people he was addressing would have revolted on the spot. He would never have had the success in his regime.

Soc: Yet this Hitler you speak of, wouldn't he have gotten farther then he did if he had been honest and truthful to his people?

Karl: Would he have? He kept from his people and even the world his strange yet powerful ways of dealing with an undesirable section of his populace. He gave a struggling and beaten country a reason to continue and to build from the ashes of World War I a country to be proud of and even a country in some sections to envy.

Soc: Yet war is a useless endeavor. To wage war against a people because of their social or economic class is futile. They can not be changed by the bludgeon nor by the fist. True change comes to the less fortunate in a society from education and enlightenment.

Karl: Yet even you say that the aspect of enlightenment through the glare of the sun from out the evils of the cave cause confusion and a state of unwillingness to accept what the eyes tell you. You even say that "perception" is something we can't even trust. Why is it then that you find the idea of truth from a lie so abhorrent? Especially if in this day and age, with the control over the media that this administration has, that the repetition of a lie enough times becoming truth? The people, because of their fear and confusion, need to be lied to, to be able to continue on with their mundane existence.

Soc: But why? Why is it that the act of a lie, repeated enough times through more then one of these "agencies" batted around through the airwaves and regurgitated out to the masses a needed thing? Why would one, one who in my mind should be more educated and understanding then the rest of the masses, be so covetous and so entrenched within the need to lie? Why not allow for the truth to be sent out, batted around those same airwaves and regurgitated to those same masses that you condescend to know what they need?

Karl: Because it's what we are elected for. It's what we're needed for by those same masses. Those pathetic adult/children of America that think they know what they need are confused and addled dolts. Pathetic losers that would be lost without us to tell them who and what to fear.

Soc: Yet within those teeming masses that you infer are lacking in not only education yet a desire to be enlightened and know the truth, are the educated and enlightened and they scream for justice to be done in dealing with this administration. Why then is there still a need for dishonesty and distrust for those same legislators that shun the truth in all its glory?

Karl: Ah, Socrates. You are naïve. It was easy in your day and age for the honest to govern and the strong to unite, yet even your own empire crumbled into dissolution and decay.

Soc: You digress Karl. I state again the question. Why in a society and culture like a "free" nation, as some would call it the great experiment, are there still those in power with a need to degrade the intelligence and the education of their own people? Why not tell the people of the strange craft in the 51st area? Why not allow then the knowledge of who assassinated the president of this same nation of the name of Kennedy? Why not allow the truth to reveal all the ills of this society so, as you put it, your own society won't crumble into dissolution and decay?

Karl: Because with the truth, the real truth, a government has the power to control the people. A few crazy's running around touting the "unfairness" of the purging of those judges, the lack of a reason for war, and all the other things we've done wouldn't serve them at all. They wouldn't know what to do with the knowledge they would receive. There would be anarchy and chaos and no one would be able to win the game of politics then.

Soc: This game as you put it is no such thing. It breathes or suffocates depending on the prowess of its leaders. You forget Karl; I too was a member of a republic at one time…

Karl: The same one that mixed you a death cocktail?

Soc: Yes. The very same. And the reasoning behind that thinking was the same as yours. A total lack of acknowledgement of the benefits to a free society and a need to corrupt the halls of power with inbreeding and god kings. And look at what that achieved? The dissolution and decay of my society 2500 years before your own. Yet you refuse to learn from its example.

Karl: Whatever. I think the stewardess left. No worries, I taped her on Beta.

Karl leaves Socrates to his musings and goes behind his section of the curtain separating the room into two halves. We leave them as they are. Socrates mixing sugar with absinthe and Karl constantly rewinding and playing certain sections of his newly acquired tape.

Works Consulted

Plato. “Allegory of the Cave.” 428-347 B.C.

Plato. “Noble Discourse” From the Phaedrus. 428-347 B.C.

For The Invisibles

Research Project

"Are you going to wear your boots? If you're dressing up, you shouldn't wear your boots."

"Do you think I don't know that homeless people are dirty?"

"Wow dude. You look scary."

While doing my research project I found very different and strange views on my work for my sociology class. Some from my family, others from individuals not only in this class, but in my other class as well. Varying views, varying positions, but all alike in one way. The lack of knowledge of these same people on the subject of the homeless.

We all know that homelessness exists. They are on street corners; they stand in the exits from shopping centers with hand made signs scrawling messages. Will work for food, homeless vet, trying to get home and out of gas. They say very little unless approached, and then because of varying degrees of mental or societal deficiencies, you could get a "normal" response to the enquiry or a string of profanity or even nonsense words strung together.

I started this research paper with a decent hypothesis. In my lack of knowledge I tried to set up my hypothesis by ensuring that a response would be had by the populous I was examining. I would dress as a typical transient, and then as an upper scale resident and as both I would scream out "monkey!" in an attempt to use ethno methodological tactics to get a desired response. I was trying to see if people actually didn't see the homeless population, or if indeed we refuse to see them. What I found was both disturbing and fascinating.

I started out in my transient garb and choose San Luis Obispo's farmer's market. Not only are the people packed into the street of Higuera, where the farmers market is held, but it allowed me to be able to get a decent cross section of the populous of San Luis Obispo so as to have a decent data collection point.

As I rubbed a collection of engine grease and tire rubbings and dirt from a flower bed on my face and hands I felt nervous. It wasn't until I had made it to Higuera that I realized I would not be able to scream "monkey" in the street, especially with the police presence, and escape with un-corrupted data. But as these thoughts ran through my head I began to notice people noticing me, and realized that I didn't need to call attention to myself at all. All I needed to do was walk the street, from one end to the other, and collect the data that was occurring around me. Without having to do anything to draw attention to myself I was getting the same reaction, I surmised, that I would have gotten if I had actually been homeless.

While in my transient garb, I quickly realized that the hypothesis I had was naive. Thinking that the homeless community needs to draw attention to itself, or even that anyone would care if they did, was the wrong direction to go. But I didn't realize this until I was in the middle of it. So I began to collect the data, for the pure sake of data collection, and I felt that I could come to some conclusion or statement that would capsulate the data I was collecting.

I was wrong.

Within my data as the transient I realized that its not that people refuse to see the homeless, or even that they don't see the homeless. It was that people noticed everything around them, even when no visual contact is made, and they choose not to acknowledge the presence of a proposed homeless person.

As a transient I was noticed, mostly by young (20-30 year old) women, and then I was *shunned.* They would look at me, and then look away. The major differences was that when they looked away, the look on their faces was either disgust or pity. And the looks of pity were few and far between. Approximately 10% or less of the women that looked at me, looked away with pity. The other 90% were disgusted.

The other interesting aspect of my transient data was that men were the only ones to acknowledge me. Either with the inevitable machismo head nod, or a slight smile. Not one woman smiled when looking at me in my transient garb. And the only two people that started up a conversation with me as a transient were people manning the booths. As I was concentrating on the eye contact of most of the people around me, I failed to notice the booths these individuals worked at.

During my transient data collection I also noticed the lack of contact that people usually encounter in farmers market, at least in this area. It's difficult to walk through this gathering of individuals without the obligatory bump by the other people there. Because of the size of the street, and the mass of people, I've never been able to walk through farmers market without being bumped. When I began to collect data as a transient I was not touched once, either by accident or by purposeful jostling. It seemed to me that people's proxemic bubbles somehow grow or become more in-tuned to the passing financial status of the people they are around. When I walked by one woman handing out pamphlets, she didn't even offer me one.

I was lucky, I realized, that I had a home, a beautiful wife, and a beautiful daughter to go to. I had a decent, yet due to the public school system of California inadequate, education. I read at least two to three books a week for recreation and have gleaned quite a lot of information from the experiences in my life. Yet none of that, beneath a thin veneer of dirt and grime, was evident to the populous at large, nor were they interested in me as a person. I was merely a filthy vagrant, to be shunned primarily because of my repugnance in dress and dirt.

After my data collection had completed I felt horrible. So in most times of need, or sadness, I resort to feeding my anguish with food. As I waited in Taco Bell, first to order, then to acquire my meal, I was stared at by a man at a booth. He was a patron of the establishment, yet his food went unnoticed because of my presence. He was, by broadcasting through his body language, disgusted by my very presence. He looked at me with such distaste I would have felt abused if not for the fact that I have a solid sense of self, and realizing my own self worth, refused his obvious attempt to intimidate me to leave. After I got home, and had my wife take a picture of me, I took a shower. I washed at least twice over my body, the first to remove the dirt, the second to remove the feeling of filth from the populous of the city I dwell in.

The next week was the week I dressed as a somewhat financially respectable person. I shaved my beard to a more restrained growth, dressed in a button up shirt and a pair of dress slacks, and did the walk yet again. I realized that as soon as I had crossed the 10 feet from one side of the street to the other and was bumped. The individual turned to me, apologized and walked on. In that moment I was amazed that the two things I ended up craving after forty minutes in my transient garb had happened in the first moments that I had entered my data collection area. In fact, before I had even gotten to my car from the class I attended that evening I had been smiled at by an older women (40-50 years of age). While dressed up I was jostled at least once, avoided being jostled another four times, and was smiled at three times, by women.

What amazed me the most, within the confines of my data collection, was that as a transient I was seen and avoided. As a "normal" middle class individual I was acknowledged more by women, yet not as much by either sex. It was as if in being like the rest of the "norms" I was almost invisible. I was accepted within their scope of understanding, primarily because of my wardrobe, yet was unnoticed by most. Whereas within my "transient" garb I was noticed by most of the people, yet I was outside the group or collective of that section of the population because of my clothing or my showering schedule.

I feel incredibly lucky being able to not only attend this class, but also in being able to become involved in this research paper. In doing this paper, and primarily the data collection, I've realized that the homeless population is not "invisible" as some reports state, nor are they hiding or even moving out of areas as others state (upi news track/ San Francisco homeless head west/May 23, 2005). The homeless population is within our communities and are actively ignored by non homeless people, not because they aren't there (Planning/ June 2005/ City Life/Harold Henderson), not because we as a nation don't see them. We actively pursue our own ignorance with abandon and an almost pathological need because of fear. That fear, of living pay check to pay check, of renting from a landlord that might not be the most affable individual, or because of our own fears started from an early age within those confines of a possible financially stressed situation. We are the reasons that there is a homeless community. We continue to allow it every time we walk by a person sitting on a street corner with a sign. Homeless people will work for food, they are veterans of foreign wars, they are our sons, and our daughters. They are not an invisible nation. They are a nation ignored, except in hushed whispers of disgust as we walk by them and realize our precarious position within our own lives. We harbor that fear, and release it when we see them huddled together for warmth and shelter. We release it when we refuse to acknowledge them except in pity and disgust. We use them as receptacles for that fear and fill them up with our lack of compassion and our lack of acknowledgment. Within the confines of the homelessness in our nation, as the old adage says, we have nothing to fear but fear itself. And that fear is within ourselves.

Pebbles in the Stream of my Consciousness

Serious proposals. Blood soaked sheets from pierced virginal brides on their only true night of fear. Demon taxi cab drivers that choose their victims ends to the chases within their lives. The construction and deconstruction of labels and criteria. My brain has ceased to swell and is now impacted like the lower bowel of an elderly opiate addict. What is the lens I've acquired and what does it all mean? As the only person in attendance at the poetry reading of a teachers friend and vicariously lived free spirit, what do I do and how do I take the only response from this "free spirit" that wishes to be that the male she had in her class called the class experience "man haters and lesbians"? Where to go and what to do?

The first stab is "Maybe an expose on the women in media and their need to be less woman when endowed with the swinging weight of pregnancy?" Instead of less woman maybe less "asskicker" was more to the point. Disney makes it a point to kill women on a regular almost serial level and the targeting of mothers specifically would eliminate some small countries in population if allowed. Then it was "Serial killers who are woman! That's it! Perfect!" I think that actually was the first one and the asskicking came after. Then it was "A stream of consciousness from Virginia Woolf during a manic episode caught on the vinyl of a record player!" Thoughts of calling it an "Edison's talking disc" flashes constantly through my mind.

Yet it all fades away into nothingness and I'm left here, at 12:38 A.M. on a Wednesday evening into a Thursday morning, and I can only derive from this experience a sinking feeling that the aspect of labels is what's at stake.

I return to the poetess.

She is hiking. She writes an essay and it comes down to being. She wants to Be. Be with capitals of course. You can hear it in her writing and it's apparent it's a "BE" if it's anything. But will she realize that she is being? Can she? Is anyone truly astute enough to be able to recognize their epiphanic moments at the time they occur? Possibly.

I find it unusual and intriguing that the total lack of labels put down about anyone else from these same women writers are heaped upon themselves. Yet as we travel forward in time we find that the women need these labels to be able to designate what it is that they truly are. We have Virginia Woolf talking of killing angels and the availability of women to seek a profession. Even before Virgy we have Kempe telling her hubby that "sans nookie" is the name of her game now and forever. And it worked. Julian telling us that in her little cell *that she asked to be put in and stored like a fragile freak* that Jesus was a woman and birthed us through his gaping wound. The ultimate in Phil Donahue show topics. If that guy could have given birth he would have.

But again, what are we supposed to take from that? What can we find within these strange scribbling of a woman in white, secluded within a house, feeding street urchins for transport? That they went the way they wanted is one central truth. They chose what they wanted and refused the path society choose for them. Kempe's disapproval and debating skills with the bishop comes to mind. They began to fear her at the end. Her power and dedication to their own feebly held beliefs were a slap of cold water for them all. More labels I see for Kempe and me.

I think of all the times I was labeled as a "father" and the fact that that label designates a man that has no idea about his children or their lives and *can't* have any idea about his children or their lives to a lot of people is startling. What sinks it home even more is the fact that every time I've had that experience it was always a woman that designated me that way. How can women or men move beyond and through this time period if we both continue to sling labels like mud at each other in a gender biased slant? The answer is we can't. Society refuses to see within itself to try to cure that aspect of our culture. Some women, I might say some women that are the most vehement about their freedom and equality, want equality but are unable to cure themselves of the knee-jerk response to men and their place within that society.

So, that said, what's the actual cure for this predicament? The total annihilation of labels. The destruction of everything gender based. Why signify women as women and men as men? Because of their sexual gear? Because ones an outy and ones an inny? Or is it because of our totally different brain wiring and the differences caused by that? What is the best way to see through all our ways and means to "get over" on others within our society to our own ends? How do we end the use and adoption of labels?

I wish I knew.

But the things I do know are in abundance and totally due to the direction of this class. I want to learn from these women, not what their gender can teach me, but what their minds can teach me. Now I'm not so naïve to believe that their being women has no bearing on their writing, of course it does. But that can't be the only reason for its exploration. It should be devoured by the mind in great gulps and bites till none remains for no reason other then its writing.

Woman or man, the sex of the creator ceases to matter when the meat of the story is "grokked", for want of a better word, in all its glory. We, as a society and a culture, need to believe in each other for the shear joy of the act itself. And the best way to do that is to believe in us all. Dickens showed us with the "God bless us everyone" moment in that singing one. Woolf, pre-rocks in the pockets, tells us continuously that the road is difficult but we must *never* cease to walk it to the end. Is that a gender specific thought? I think not.

Hemmingway gives us manly man angles in his writing at all times. It seemed like he killed the story on the page with minimalist fervor. Poe was depressed and a raving drunk off of one shot a day. Heinlein wanted nothing more then to have open marriages and a definite relaxed view on sexuality. Are we as a society to say that these feelings and thoughts are inherently male? Are women the only nurturers, because someone should have told Gilman. All of our problems and distress come from each gender specifying what the other needs to be. Why should women walk behind men and why should men dirty their outerwear on mud puddles? My son looks great in pink and my daughter looks great in blue, but due to societal ineptitude in designation of gender to androgynous youth forms, even their *clothing* designates who they are and the label they have to carry even before they realize the existence of the society they are entered into because of the sexual gratification of their parents.

Break all labels.

Shatter all the preconceptions of your life and allow for you to be you. For who you are and what you can do. Not for who you should be or what you need to fit into.

I'm off to dress my son in pink and my daughter in a blue suit with a tie.

The Terror of Terrorism

A scene opens. An old weathered mans face is seen close up. As the camera pans backward, he straightens from his hard labor in the sun and the dirt, pushes out his lower back with the hand not holding the hoe. His attention is drawn towards the sun, to a hillside and his careworn yet enigmatic face shifts from comfortable "work is nigh done" to stark abject horror. As the camera pans over to the hillside, out of a setting sun, we see the face of the (insert terrorist here).

It's an amazing thing to just type in the word "Terrorist" in a search engine. Its little gerbil parts run around for a second and out of the ether of wires and computers and storage comes this strange collection of terms. Lovely Wikipedia, the most flexible information on the net today, tells us "Someone who engages in terrorism" is a terrorist. Dictionary.com tells us "(formerly) a member of a political group in Russia aiming at the demoralization of the government". On YouTube it's a collection of "The World's Wildest Terrorist Video Bloopers. (If you like it, consider subscribing. You'll be the first to know when we upload new videos.)" , even a "Terrorist Attack Survival Kit CD $29.99. Hosted by Kelly Perdew West Point Graduate, former U.S. Army Airborne Ranger and winner of "The Apprentice" TV Show."

Now why would America allow its media to engage the fear response so strongly? And to truly what end? Fear is the best way to control a population. If the country in question uses a *nameless* or *faceless* fear, even better. Now your populous, at least the ones listening to your government controlled, or at the least heavily governmentally influenced media, can watch as the threat grows, then falls, then grows, then falls. But it never has gone to green. We'll never be safe.

When we all look back to the Regan era we have the old man rising from his productive crouch to see "DRUGS" marauding down the hillside. In the era of WWII we have the fear of the Japanese and their internment at Manzanar. As well as most other Asiatic peoples because they, the government, didn't know the difference between a Korean, a Pilipino, or even a person of Chinese descent.

Who truly is a terrorist? A terrorist is someone who, through the actions or deeds of them or their organization, causes terror in the population they are in conflict with and are also living in. So with this one word, as a nation and a people, we can envelope anyone we want. Our Bill of Rights tells us quite elegantly exactly what those rights are, yet there are people held at Guantanamo. Amnesty International has a whole litany of human rights violations that go on that place up to and including people being seized before the age of 18 in foreign countries, or the fact that there has never been a conviction of anyone at Guantanamo by the United States. They also state that out of the 775 detainees held at Guantanamo there have been 40 suicide attempts reported. That's 20% of the detainee population is trying to die as a way out of that place.

Where do we go now? Its been some time since the threat level meter has reared its ugly head so maybe with all the hullabaloo from the people at Amnesty, along with others, have gotten some point across. Ashcroft is gone, Rumsfield has gone, the terror threat level with the constant warnings and action reports from the front has died away. The bumper stickers to "Impeach Bush and Cheney" are cropping up everywhere. Yet even with a lot more attention being given to human rights losses and trampled dignity, can we truly as a people close down, as Amnesty wants, a place to put those people that are undoubtedly terrorists? Can we as a nation be so naïve as to believe if we don't do something about terrorism it will just go away? So we need to find a middle ground, a "happy medium".

The justice department should begin trying or extraditing for trial those individuals actually caught in an act or the commission of an act of terrorism. Try them with judges and juries and give then the same chances that everyone has. If they are brought to us from other countries, and we pay those other countries for those prisoners (Amnesty again) we should stop that practice. The countries that bring us their political prisoners should be made to try their own. Unless it is directly and specifically an attack against the United States, we don't house their offal any more. Or if we need to, for security for an ally of something, we charge them a fee for housing these criminals and form a contract that would state that the country had to bring said prisoner to trial by such and such a date and if not the prisoner is sent back, and make that COD please.

We have a collection of individuals, some terrorists, some not, that need to be either tried or released to their respective governments. The information held by the governments in question, the United States as well, needs to come out and the trials need to occur for the public to be able to form their own decision about terrorism and terrorists. And our country needs to be held responsible for its misdeeds. We need to get back to what it truly means to be an American and live in the land of the free. That means freedom from our terror of the terrorists and freedom from ourselves.

Work's Cited

Wikipedia. "Terrorist". Online Posting. http://en.wikipedia.org/wiki/Terrorist.16 May 2007

terrorist." *Dictionary.com Unabridged (v 1.1)*. Random House, Inc. 17 May. 2007. <Dictionary.com http://dictionary.reference.com/browse/terrorist>.

Poykpac. "Terrorist Bloopers". Online Video.http://youtube.com/watch?v=w57JLmY5dmw

American Family Protection Inc. “Terrorist Attack Survival Kit”. http://www.terroristattackcd.com/

Amnesty International. “Close Guantanamo USA, Guantanamo in Numbers” http://web.amnesty.org/library/Index/ENGAMR511862006. 8 December, 2006

On The Prospect Of Death

I cruise in my Toyota truck up highway one. I'm heading home after a night of some serious partying. I've been at a friend's house for most of the evening and am somewhat unsuccessfully trying to keep the inevitable Mr. Sandman at bay for a few more moments. I curve slightly left following the gradual turn that will take me past the San Luis County Jail and my new Alma Matter. I'm almost home and my mind starts to drift. I begin to think of the paper that's due in my English 56 class. I shoot past the jail and am almost to my scholastic way point when I am violently vaulted into pristine consciousness.

I've moved past the first exit and headed for the turn off for Rancho El Chorro when a tan/orange blur quickly crosses my path. My hands involuntarily grip the wheel and jerk it slightly to the right. My breathing escalates and my vision clears. The fog that had been growing as the shots had kept coming is roughly thrown to the back of my brain. I am now fully awake. As I sit bolt upright on the bench seat my mind flashes to....

I'm nineteen, almost twenty, and am serving my country in the land of beer and women. I'd volunteered for active duty in the European theatre because my financial income had been somewhat lacking. I was an E3, a private first class, and figured some active duty pay and benefits would go well together. So, off to the barber for a puritanical haircut and two weeks in an almost labor camp atmosphere in a National Guard base and I was on the plane. The unit I became attached to, the 470th MP Co flew into Reinmein Air force base in the wee morning hours of December 23. We got set up in barracks and began our tour.

The seven months I spent in Germany were by far the strangest and yet most interesting of my life. I saw and experienced many things in that rustic and learned culture but in the flash I only saw a snapshot.

I can't remember my partners name anymore. He was the kind of guy that might trek all over Mexico to find the immortal donkey show, and then complain that he'd seen better. I remember waking up in my four man room to the sight of him smiling over me with a huge bowl of chili beans. Later on the" who could make the other guy roll down the window for fear of methane asphyxiation" contest would begin. Needless to say he almost always won.

We had been patrolling in the residential section of the base I was stationed on for about a month or so and things had been fairly smooth. Other than in basic training I had never done actual patrol work of any kind on the street. The unit that was my actual duty station was mostly a combat oriented unit so the whole "street cop" format had escaped me. That in itself was an impact on me psychologically. Here I was not even old enough for a bar back home yet I could walk into bars, porno theatres, strip clubs, and pretty much most other forms of debauchery laced activities. The part that made me nervous was that I had been given a gun.

My partner and I are following a VW van. The van swerves as our roof lights come on, but doesn't stop. We follow him for awhile and eventually he stops, with most of the car at a healthy slant to the roadside.

Even before my overzealous partner can get out of the patrol car, the guy jumps out of the car and starts back to the patrol vehicle cursing and gesturing wildly. My partner gets out on his side of the VW van that served as our patrol car and instructs the man to please return to his car. I of course follow his lead and exit from my side. The man apparently doesn't hear us and continues his tirade. I hear my partner repeat his request with a bit more inflection and I look over at him. His cover on his sidearm is unsnapped. I quickly unsnap my holster and look back at the man.

Now it is important for me to be able to convey to you that I was very green. I was the ultimate rookie. I had almost no real patrol experience and in life experience I was also somewhat lacking. The only thing I had was an active imagination and an over abundance of frightening information. Information that dictated that most police officers die in routine traffic stops than in any other police incursions into the general populous. The only other information I had were training films. One in particular flashed into my head at that moment.

An orange county police officer had pulled a gentleman over on a routine traffic stop and the man had exited his car, gone to the back of his vehicle, opened the trunk and pulled a revolver on the officer. The man had turned to the officer and pulled the trigger. The safety was on. The officer had subsequently shot the man to death.

The man was still moving toward us shouting profanities. The picture of me and my partner dead kept flashing in my head. I turn to look at my partner and he's drawn his sidearm. He tells the man to return to his car "right now". I pull my sidearm and aim center mass, somewhere at the mans chest. I begin a litany in my head, almost a mantra. I pray to whatever or whoever holy that this man will return to his vehicle so I won't have to shoot him. I know the hole that a .45 shell can do to a human body. The man is almost to the hood of the patrol vehicle. My partner reiterates his strident request as I flip the safety off my pistol, and the man backs off. Maybe he realized the situation or maybe it was just the dumb luck of fools, but I was not forced to kill for fear of my or my partner's safety.

I'm back in my truck. I pass the last exit to Cuesta and my truck follows the winding path home. I flash to a more recent memory.

I'm driving back with my girlfriend and a close friend of mine from painted rock in the Carrizo plains. Its evening and the night is without a moon. My girlfriends Jeep Wrangler is eating up the road when the headlights pick out a form in the distance. A doe, a deer, a female deer as the song goes, is by the right side of the road. I slow the jeep to allow her to cross to the other side. The deer begins to run alongside the road in the same direction as the vehicle, almost keeping pace. I slow further now fairly concerned. The deer turns quickly to the left, cutting off the vehicle. The thirty five mile an hour impact picks up her hind section and spin lifts her counter clockwise and out of the light of the headlamps. I bring the car to a halt. The same enlivening aspects of fear spread through my body as I back the jeep up. The only thought I have is a slim hope that the deer is already dead. I pull the Buck knife that is strapped to my waist that I wear when I hike and walk out of the light produced by the car. The deer is nowhere to be found.

I'm back in my truck driving once again towards home. I realize whether through insight or moral obligations that death is the same in any situation. Be it a drunk and belligerent man that dies on the streets of an American base in Germany by the hand of a police officer, or a deer that's sustained so much damage to its body that it only has strength to find a place to die in peace. Death is not romantic. Death is not cool. Death is absolute and can never be taken back. Orwell understood, yet was too weak to stop the engine of death from consuming his soul. So far I've been lucky. I hope I keep my innocence a while longer.

The Last Abortion Clinic

Disturbing. That was the first, and the last feeling this assignment brought out of me.

While watching the "Frontline" program I was hard pressed to keep my head from shaking in disbelief. I was amazed at the cunning and underhanded way in which the pro-life groups are now, and have been, working the lobbyist angle within the hallowed halls of the courts, not only within the states represented, but also within the specific state of Mississippi.

The pro-lifers seem to want to stop abortion not, as they specify, because of women's health issues, but because they feel abortion is wrong due to their religious beliefs. And the plot thickens from there. These same people who are so "concerned" with the women's health they are trying to help do not concentrate on the pre or even post natal health. They bring you into a nice little house, somewhere in a low-income area where that same said house is probably the best one in the neighborhood, and pray for the mother and child. They refuse to give out abortion clinics numbers, or even to ensure that the mothers, many of them teens, get decent care for themselves and their unborn children. I can't state enough times how truly reprehensible this programs content was to me. I'm glad

I actually got a chance to see this program, and the information involved was comprehensive, yet the way that these same people that are "trying to save a baby" stand in front of a clinic that not only supplies the chance for an abortion to women, but also have other services for women and men. Most of the planned parenthood clinics, thanks to our guest speaker, stated that not only are abortions available within the clinic, they also have birth control and other services available to their clientele. Which begs the question, are the loss of these clinics within the specific state of Mississippi also causing the rise of teen pregnancy? Because of a lack, presumably throughout the entire state of Mississippi, of clinics that are non religious based, is that causing the availability of contraception to decrease? The "Pregnancy Crisis Centers" have no birth control services. They have no actual pre or post natal care for either the mother or the child. They only allow a single ultrasound, then pray and send the mother on her way, usually with a pack of oversized diapers and a can or two of formula. I call this irresponsible and negligent to their populous.

I also found it interesting that most of the pro-lifers and even the people working at these "crisis" centers are predominately white middle to upper class people. I found it interesting that they could stand outside the clinic in Clarksville day after day and yell at the women seeking help from the clinic, yet are able to wear expensive suit outfits to lobby for tighter abortion control. I was wondering through most of that program, where are they when the child is born? Where are they when the mothers of these children need financial, occupational, or medical help? It seems they are outside the clinic, harassing the clientele that's just trying to get the medical treatments that are their right by federal law.

In response to the questions asked for this paper, I feel that the federal government should stop creating amendments to the statutes that are already on the books. Abortion should be a federally mandated right throughout the states regardless of that states religious views. The fact that the Supreme Court can mandate the statutes about this issue, and then back pedal for religious extremist groups is abhorrent.

In the opinions of the kids interviewed in the "shifting attitudes" I think that their responses are direct results of the abstinence programs instituted within their states. Because of that, and the reading I was able to do for my section of the "tiny teach "section of our class, I realized that these poor girls really didn't have all the facts available to them. The one girl was even ambiguous on the way the morning after pill worked calling it repeatedly the "abortion" pill. This after she also stated that the kids in the discussion were "all intelligent women". I think that they were able to sit there in that room and remark about the "moral" and "ethical" reasons behind their on positions, yet they had no information to back it up. They would state their pro-choice views in extreme pro-life ways, then refute themselves with the statements that they "had no idea. I mean, if it was illegal we wouldn't be having this discussion. We can't know what it was like before it [abortion] was legal." They also kept returning to the fact that their generation seems to be swinging more to the conservative sides of these issues. I can't think of one person I know, except the crazy roommate of an ex-girlfriend, that was so promiscuous as to have multiple partners within a single weekend. After the said weekend, the guy was rushed out of the house, then the “cut-down” would begin. She would extol on the lack of virtues of her most recent sexual partner. What surprised me, and seemed to run through the attitudes within the kids in the discussion, was that it’s no longer about searching for a special person to be able to not only love and cherish, but respect. It seems to be about the “hook-up” culture. The girls within the discussion seemed to have no issue with casual sex, even with multiple partners, yet when the discussion turned to abortion they would all have the children. A few would seek adoption, but the bulk of them would have the children. Yet they don't necessarily know what that entails. These kids even have casual sex, yet have problems talking about the outcome of the acts their engaging in. Only one girl stated that she has the discussion about the male’s views on abortion with her prospective partner before the act itself.

It's at least slightly reassuring that within those discussions they all felt the need for the availability of legal abortion, yet their cavalier attitude about their sexual practices surprised and distressed me. I don't think I know of a single female that would wish abortion to be illegal, yet because of the span of time between the true feminist movement and now we have lost our way politically on these issues. Roe v. Wade seems to have made our country roll over and go back to sleep thinking that all is right in the world, while our lives are being reprogrammed by the pro-lifers in their lobbying for their own religious agendum.

www.ingramcontent.com/pod-product-compliance
Lightning Source LLC
Chambersburg PA
CBHW020944310726
48980CB00001B/41

9780615261928